The Change

Even the book morphs!
Flip the pages
and check it out!

Look for other **ANIMORPHS**™
titles by K.A. Applegate:

the andalite chronicles

ANIMORPHS™

The Change

K.A. Applegate

AN
APPLE
PAPERBACK

SCHOLASTIC INC.
New York Toronto London Auckland Sydney

For Michael

Cover illustration by David B. Mattingly

ISBN 0-590-49418-X

10 9 8 7 6 5 4 3 2 1   7 8 9/9 0 1 2/0

Printed in the U.S.A.   40

First Scholastic printing, December 1997

CHAPTER 1

My name is Tobias.

The other Animorphs can't tell you very much about themselves, but I can. See, I don't have an address. I can't be found. I live in an area of forest by a meadow. That's my territory.

My territory includes the meadow, which is maybe a hundred yards across in one direction, and half that in the other direction. My territory also includes the trees around the meadow, and the woods heading north for about another hundred yards.

Of course, my territory is also the territory of other animals. Owls, jays, foxes, raccoons, on down to ants and spiders. But no red-tailed hawks.

Except me.

My name is Tobias, and I am human. Partly. Most of my mind is human. At least I think it is. I mean, I remember human things. I can read and use language. Most of my close friends are human. And I was born a human, in a human body with arms and legs and hair and a mouth.

Now, though, I have wings and talons and feathers. And instead of a mouth I have a hooked beak.

I can make sounds with my beak. But nothing that sounds human. To speak with regular humans I use thought-speak.

But there were no people nearby right then in the early morning, as I waited patiently in the branch of a dying elm tree.

I kept my eyes focused sharply on the meadow. I knew the pathways and homes of the mice and rats and rabbits who lived there. And I knew what it meant when the tall, dry grass twitched just the smallest bit.

With my hawk's eyes I could see what no human could hope to see. I could see the individual stalks of grass barely tremble as a mouse brushed between them.

And with my hawk's ears I heard the faint sound of mouse teeth, chewing on a seed.

The mouse was seventy or eighty feet away. An easy target.

I opened my wings slowly, not wanting to make a sound. I released the grip of my talons on the branch and fell forward. My wings caught the cushion of air and I swooped, almost silent, toward my prey.

The grass twitched.

Through the grass I saw a flash of brown. The mouse was running.

Too slowly.

I raked my talons forward. I swept my wings forward to cancel my speed, dropped one wing to turn, and fell the last foot like a rock.

It was all over very quickly.

But this time as I dragged the mouse away to a safer spot, I stumbled on a faded magazine someone had thrown away. The wind whipped the pages by, one at a time. Advertisements. Graphs. Pictures of the president with some foreign leader.

And then one page stayed open. A photograph of a classroom. Kids my age. Some of the kids were goofing off in the back of the class. Some looked bored. Most looked more or less interested, and three were practically leaping from their seats, waving their hands for the teacher. All that, frozen in a photograph.

A classroom like any classroom. Like the classrooms I used to attend. I would have been one of the kids paying attention, but too shy to

volunteer. I was never very bold or aggressive. I was a bully-magnet, to tell you the truth. The kid most likely to get pounded. The kid from the home so screwed up that I ended up being shuttled back and forth between aunts and uncles who didn't even remember my name half the time.

But that wasn't me anymore.

CHAPTER 2

This is my life now. I accept it. And there are some very nice things about being a bird.

Some *very* nice things.

Well-fed and full of energy, I flapped across the meadow, gaining altitude the hard way — with sheer muscle power.

I swept above the trees and fought my way higher still. Out beyond my own territory. Higher and higher. And then I felt the air billowing up beneath me.

A beautiful thermal. A pillar of warm air that rose up from the ground as it was heated by the sun. I swept into that warm air and it lifted me up like an elevator.

I turned and turned within that warm current,

twisting higher and higher, till I was nothing but a speck to the tiny humans on the ground. Up and up, till the only sound was the wind ruffling across my feathers.

I caught a glimpse back down behind me. A glimpse of a strange creature that looked like a blue deer at first. Until you saw the head with its extra stalk eyes mounted on top. And the slashing, scorpion tail.

Aximili-Esgarrouth-Isthill. The only Andalite alive on Earth. My friend. Or as much of a friend as you can be, when one of you is a Bird-boy and the other is an alien.

<Ax-man!> I called down. He kept running. That's how he eats. He runs across grass and leaves, and the crushed vegetation is absorbed up through his hooves.

<Tobias! Out hunting?>

<Nope. I had breakfast. See you later.>

I flapped and glided and soared till I was over houses. They were just little squares of gray and orange and brown roofs. Tiny swimming pools glittered an unnatural blue. I saw trimmed green lawns and parked rectangles of cars and roads with dotted white lines down the middle.

I flew on, across the homes, across the roads, to the school. Maybe it was because of the picture in the magazine. Maybe that's why I wanted to go there.

It was late morning now. The light was sharp and clean. I could see through the windows of the classrooms.

There was Jake, unofficial leader of the Animorphs, looking like any normal guy. He was lounging at his desk, feet stuck out in front. He was sleepy and trying to keep his eyes open.

More than any other person alive, Jake held the future of the human race in his hands. Strange to think, huh? That some big, sleepy kid in sneakers and a jacket was the leader of the only resistance to the Yeerk invasion of Earth?

As I watched, he nodded twice and slumped. The girl sitting behind him leaned forward and gave him a gentle poke in the shoulder.

That was Cassie. Another member of our little group. Cassie has never met an animal she didn't like. And she's never met a fashion she cared about. She's small, compact but strong-looking. Not like she's muscular. More like she's part of something bigger than herself. Like she's some living extension of the earth.

Anyway, that's how I see her. Like some gentle soldier in the service of nature itself. Corny, isn't it? Sorry, but I have a lot of time to think. And I guess that makes me get too serious sometimes.

I swept by, high above, and turned the corner. In another classroom I spotted Marco. He was

7

talking. This was not a surprise. The class began to laugh. The teacher laughed, too, then looked exasperated, like she didn't want to laugh. This was also not a surprise. That's Marco. The boy loves to be the center of attention.

It took a while before I spotted the last human member of the Animorphs. She wasn't in her usual classroom. In fact, I spotted her first in just a brief glimpse, walking down the hall.

Then she stepped outside. Out into the empty quad that separated the main building from the gym and the temporary buildings.

She stepped out into the sunlight, and her blond hair became a flame of pure gold.

Rachel.

Have you ever known a person who seems to walk through life with her own private spotlight shining on her? That's Rachel.

<Hi,> I said in thought-speak. <What are you doing? Skipping school?>

She couldn't answer. See, you can only do thought-speak when you're in a morph (or if you happen to be an Andalite). Although you can hear it just fine.

Rachel stopped walking and shielded her eyes with her hand, scanning the sky for me. Then she gave just the smallest wave, just a twinkling of two fingers.

She jerked her head toward the gym. That's where she was going. She opened her binder and revealed a piece of yellow notepaper clipped inside. Ah, so she was delivering a note for some teacher.

But Rachel must have forgotten that I can see things no human could ever see. Beneath the note was a fancy-looking sheet of stationery. It was a letter, addressed to Rachel. It read: "Congratulations! You have been named a Packard Foundation Outstanding Student."

I was about to add my own congratulations, when I noticed the date. There was to be an awards ceremony Monday. This was Friday. It was the kind of thing Rachel would have invited everyone to.

Everyone but me. I can't exactly go to things like awards ceremonies. Rachel hadn't even told me about it. And I knew why.

<Hey, I have something to show you after school,> I said, trying to sound perky. <My Yeerk pool mapping project is paying off. Want to go for a fly after last period?>

I saw her smile. She nodded her head again, just a slight movement no one else would notice.

<Cool,> I said.

I soared away and she walked on to the gym.

There are definitely some nice things about

9

being a hawk. And flying with Rachel is probably the nicest. But it would have been nice to see her get the Packard award, too.

Sometimes I asked myself if I had it to do all over again. . . . If I could never become Tobias the hawk, and only be Tobias the boy, would I actually do it?

I didn't think about that often, though. Maybe I didn't want to find out the answer.

CHAPTER 3

I spent the day drifting around on the breeze and checking everything I had learned in the last couple of weeks.

See, we knew the Yeerk pool was a gigantic underground complex beneath the school. We knew it extended at least as far as the mall. But we had never figured out where all the entrances and exits were.

That's what I'd been doing with my days — following people we knew were Controllers, watching them come and go. From them I learned the extent of the Yeerk pool.

Maybe I should back up and explain. I know you're probably someone living a nice, normal life. You go to school, hang out with your friends,

have dinner with your family, watch a little TV. Normal.

And if I told you that maybe your teachers aren't really your teachers anymore; and maybe your friends aren't your friends at all; and maybe even your parents have become something totally different, well, you might think I was nuts.

I understand. You wouldn't believe how often I have these dreams that maybe none of it's real. That there is no Yeerk invasion. That Yeerk slugs are not inside the heads of so many people. That maybe I have my own hands and toes. . . .

It all started when Jake, Cassie, Marco, Rachel, and I took a different way home from the mall. In a dark, eerie, abandoned construction site we saw the spaceship land. And we met the strange part-deer, part-scorpion, part-humanoid creature called an Andalite.

His name was Elfangor. Much later we found out he was Ax's big brother.

He told us about the Yeerks, the race of parasitic slugs. The Yeerks, who, like some awful galactic disease, are spreading secretly from planet to planet.

They steal bodies. They make other creatures into Controllers — absolute slaves. The entire Hork-Bajir race has been enslaved. As well as the incredibly gross Taxxons, although they went along voluntarily. They've gotten the Gedds and other races, too.

And now, it's our turn.

They are here. The Yeerks are among us. Inside the people you least suspect. Cops. Teachers. Friends. Parents. Reporters. Pastors and priests. Your own brothers and sisters.

The Andalite Prince Elfangor warned us. And he gave us the weapon — the power to morph. To become any animal we could touch and acquire.

There was just one big drawback, see. You can't stay in a morph for more than two hours. After that you stay in morph forever. That's what happened to me.

The Yeerks also have a weakness. Every three days they have to return to the Yeerk pool. They drain out of the heads of their host bodies and swim in the sludgy liquid of the pool. There they soak up the Kandrona rays that they must have for nutrition.

We've been to the Yeerk pool. It's not a place you want to see. Trust me. The screams that we'd heard in that place will be with me forever.

The Yeerk pool was where I lost my humanity. Where I passed the fateful two-hour time limit. Someday, somehow, we will destroy that place. But first, we have to understand it better.

That's what I was doing. That's why I spent

my days trying to discover every possible way in and out of it.

I was in the air over the mall at just about two-thirty in the afternoon when I spotted the big bald eagle floating, serene and powerful, on the thermals. The brown body stood out against the clouds, while the white head seemed almost invisible.

It was an odd place for a baldie. They usually like the shore.

I flapped hard to change direction and gain speed toward the eagle. I knew this eagle.

<Is that you, Rachel?> I asked.

<Sure. Who else would it be? Is this great flying weather, or what?>

<It's perfect. You up for a little cruise?>

<Of course. What's up?>

<Well, while you and the others have been off saving the world, I've been busy, too.>

I shot by, just beneath Rachel's big eagle wings, and swung out past her, then turned and moved in front of her. I was showing off. I'm more agile in the air than a bald eagle is. Although a baldie is quite a bit bigger than me. Kind of like comparing a turkey to a chicken.

Rachel made a sighing sound in my head. <Tobias, just because you can't come along on every single mission doesn't mean you need to do extra work.>

<Yeah, well, whatever,> I said. <The point is I've been watching known Controllers from the air. I started with Chapman and his wife and the reporter and the policewoman we know about. And Tom, of course.>

Chapman is our assistant principal. He's a very big deal Controller. Tom is Jake's brother. He's a Controller, too.

<I followed them and watched them and now I've found four separate ways into the Yeerk pool. Besides the one we know that goes through the mall.>

<Cool. When we know the Yeerk pool entrances, we can start figuring out who more Controllers are.> Rachel sounded impressed. Even though all I'd done was fly around and keep my eyes open.

<I have a lot of free time,> I said. I knew I shouldn't say what I was about to say next. But it was out before I could stop myself. <So. Congratulations, I guess, huh? Packard Foundation Outstanding Student.>

Rachel was silent for a few seconds. <Did someone tell you? Oh, no, of course not. You saw the letter in my notebook.>

<Just call me old hawkeye,> I said lightly.

<Tobias . . . you know how much I wish you could come. I mean, Cassie will be there, and she's great. But you know Marco will just be mak-

15

ing snide remarks, and Jake will be trying not to laugh.>

<No big deal,> I said. <The only thing is, don't hide stuff from me because you think it will hurt my feelings, okay? I can't handle you feeling sorry for me.>

<I don't feel sorry for you,> Rachel lied.

<Good. Because, you know, how you think about me is sort of important.>

I winced. I'd sounded way too sincere.

I mean, what was I thinking? Rachel's a human. A real human. I'm a hawk. You think Romeo and Juliet were doomed, just from being from families that didn't like each other? Well, you can't get any more doomed than caring for someone who isn't even the same species.

<Anyway, congratulations,> I said as breezily as I could.<Now follow me, and I'll give you a little tour of the Yeerk pool entrances.>

<On a day like this, I'd follow you anywhere,> Rachel said.

CHAPTER 4

<We're not going far. Just to the car wash.>

<They're using the car wash? No way.> Rachel laughed. <You have to admit, they are ingenious.>

We flew. Not side by side, because that would have looked suspicious. Hawks and eagles don't exactly fly in formation like geese. We kept a hundred yards apart. But with our incredible vision and thought-speak, we might as well have been next to each other.

We rose higher and higher on the thermals, then thermal-hopped. That's where you rise to the top of one pillar of warm air and glide to the next. Then you rise again and drift to the next. It's an easy, lazy kind of flying. You don't get

where you're going very fast, but you don't get tired out, either.

It was awfully nice, flying just under the bellies of the clouds with Rachel. I may have lost my human body. But I've gained wings. And flying is . . . well, I'm sure you've daydreamed about it. I know I used to. I'd sit in class, gazing out at the sky, or lie back in the grass, looking up, and wonder what it would be like to have wings. To be able to fly up and up and away from all the stupid little problems of life.

Flying is as wonderful as you'd think. It has problems, too, like anything else. But oh man, on a warm day with the mountains of fluffy white clouds showing the way to the thermal updrafts, it's just wonderful.

<So where are we going? We're not heading toward the car wash,> Rachel pointed out.

I snapped alert. I looked down at the ground, spotting the familiar road grids and buildings I knew so well from this angle. We were in an area bordering the forest. Not far from Cassie's farm. <What am I doing *here*?> I asked. <I must have spaced. Sorry. This way.>

I cranked a hard left turn and beat my wings to gain some speed. Rachel has to deal with the two-hour limit. We'd wasted a lot of that time. I couldn't believe I'd spaced out so badly.

We flapped hard for a while.

18

<Um . . . Tobias? Am I crazy, or are we right back where we were?>

I looked down at the ground. She was right. We were right back in the same area by the edge of the forest.

I felt a cold chill. <No way,> I whispered.

<Are you lost?>

<Lost? Of course not,> I said. <I don't get lost. We're heading just south of east. I know exactly where we are. But this isn't where I was heading.>

<Is there something going on here?> Rachel asked.

<This makes no sense,> I said. <I was heading for —>

And that's when I saw it happen.

We were gliding over the edge of the forest. Farmland on one side, all green and perfectly squared. Then a band of scruffy brush and fallen-down wire fence. Then the trees — elms, oaks, various pines.

The trees extended in a long sweep right, from the farmland up into the far-distant mountains. With my hawk's vision I could even see snow on those far-off peaks.

But that's not what I was noticing right then. What I was noticing right then was that a single huge oak tree was sliding to one side.

Just sliding. Like it had no roots. Like it was

on a skateboard or something. A huge oak tree just slid over.

And beneath the oak there appeared a hole in the ground.

<What is *that*?> Rachel demanded.

<You got me,> I said.

<That whole tree is just . . . moving.>

<And the hole under it isn't natural,> I pointed out. <It's too round. It's man-made.>

<Or else not *man*-made,> Rachel said darkly.

<Something's down there! I saw something moving. It's coming up! Coming up out of the ground!>

<I see it,> Rachel said. <What is it? Can you see?>

I had a better angle than Rachel. And I could see what was coming up from underground.

I saw a snakelike head with huge forward-swept horns.

I saw powerful shoulders and arms that were armed with blades at the elbows and wrists.

I saw the big Tyrannosaurus feet and the short, spiked tail and the blades at the knees.

I saw seven feet of razor-bladed death.

<Hork-Bajir,> I said.

CHAPTER 5

<Hork-Bajir!> Rachel snarled.

A year ago that name would have meant nothing to me. It would have just been some nonsense word.

But now I knew the Hork-Bajir. The Andalite who gave us our powers had told us that the Hork-Bajir were once a decent, peaceful species. But they had been enslaved by the Yeerks. All of them were Controllers now. The entire species carried the Yeerk slugs in their heads.

And with the Yeerks controlling their every action, the Hork-Bajir were walking killing machines.

Amazingly fast. Incredibly strong. Armored,

bladed, almost fearless. They were the shock troops of the Yeerk empire.

Hork-Bajir had come close to killing Rachel several times. And all of us had felt the Hork-Bajir blades at least once.

<What is a Hork-Bajir doing, coming out in broad daylight?> Rachel asked.

I looked closely. The Hork-Bajir was climbing some kind of ladder. When it reached the surface, it blinked its reptilelike eyes at the light. It climbed out and stood like some vision of a demon. Then I noticed that there was a second Hork-Bajir coming up behind it.

<There are two of them!> Rachel said.

<Yeah. And you know what? I think they look scared.>

Just then . . .

SKREEEET! SKREEEET! SKREEEET!

The alarm was deafening to my hawk hearing. The sound screamed up from the hole in the ground. The two Hork-Bajir jerked in surprise and fear. One of them grabbed the other and held it close for a split second. In an instant, they were off and running through the forest.

Running as if their lives depended on it.

And let me tell you something — Hork-Bajir can move out when they want. Those big, long legs take big, long steps. They plowed into the brush, slashing wildly with their bladed arms, slicing through bushes and thorns and small trees like a harvester going through a wheat field.

<How are you doing on morph time?> I asked Rachel.

<I still have an hour at least,> she said.

<So we follow these guys?>

<Oh, yeah.>

We flapped to gain some of the altitude we'd lost and prepared to follow the Hork-Bajir. Not much of a challenge, really. They were chopping a path straight through the woods that a blind man could follow.

<They're not exactly into the stealth thing, are they?> Rachel commented.

And that's when things really broke loose. Up from the hole in the ground humans poured. Armed humans. Men and women, dressed in an array of normal-looking human clothing.

Controllers, of course. Not that you could tell by looking. But I knew now that hole led down to the Yeerk pool. And there was no doubt in my mind — these humans were human-Controllers. Slaves to the Yeerks in their heads.

They carried human weapons — automatic rifles, handguns, shotguns.

The Yeerks were going after the two Hork-Bajir. But they were being careful. They were

sending only human-Controllers. They weren't going to risk any more Hork-Bajir being seen by normal people.

Twenty . . . thirty human-Controllers climbed up out of the hole.

<They'll never catch them,> Rachel said.

<I know. What is going on here? Are those Hork-Bajir trying to escape somehow?>

Up from the hole, machines began to appear. They seemed to levitate. I almost laughed when I saw them.

<Dirt bikes? The Yeerks have motorcycles?> It seemed bizarre, even funny. The Yeerks have faster-than-light spacecrafts. Now they were using dirt bikes?

<Uh-oh,> Rachel said. <The Hork-Bajir are fast, but they aren't *that* fast.>

VrrrrRRRROOOM! VrrrrRRRROOOM! Vrrrr-RRRROOOOM!

Human-Controllers were firing up the motorcycles. I could hear the sputtering roar of the engines. In all, fifteen Yamahas and Kawasakis came up through that hole.

VrrrrRRRROOOM! Vrrrrraaaa-vrrrraaa-vraaaa!

The motorcycles took off. Some had just one rider. Others had two — one to steer and one to shoot.

The Hork-Bajir had a lead of a few hundred yards, but they'd never outrun this small army.

As I watched from the safety of the air above, the motorcycles roared off through the woods in pursuit. They churned up dirt and leaves and shattered the quiet.

And they gained quickly on the two fleeing Hork-Bajir.

BLAM! BLAM! BLAM! BLAM!

Rifles barked. Motorcycles roared! The Hork-Bajir ran, but the bikes leaped and twisted and snaked toward them.

BLAM! BLAM! BLAM!

BAMBAMBAMBAMBAMBAMBAMBAM!

Rifles, automatic weapons, and shotguns all ripped apart the tree trunks. The human-Controllers were firing wildly. Firing at anything that moved. From the ground they couldn't see the Hork-Bajir yet. But they could see flashes of them, and they kept on shooting.

<This is going to be all over in about ten seconds,> Rachel said grimly. <What are we going to do?>

<You want to help Hork-Bajir?> I asked incredulously.

<Have you ever heard the saying, "The enemy of my enemy is my friend"? The Yeerks want these two Hork-Bajir dead. That's good enough for me.>

<Me, too,> I said. <We'll have to use thought-speak. Talk directly to them.>

<Let's do it,> Rachel said.

I would have smiled if I'd had a mouth. Rachel is so brave she is just short of being reckless.

I like that about her.

<Hey. Hork-Bajir down there.>

I saw them stagger, as though they were shocked and amazed to be hearing thought-speak. Like *that* was their major problem.

<You're about ten seconds away from being dead,> I said. <Listen to me and you just might get out of this alive.>

CHAPTER 6

<First of all, stop tearing up the foliage, ge-niuses. They're following the trail you make. And second of all . . . jump left! Now! *Jump!*>

The two Hork-Bajir leaped to their left, just as a pair of motorcycles roared past, missing them by a few feet.

BOOM! BOOM!

One of the Controllers cut loose with both bar-rels of a shotgun. I could see the pellets tear a tree trunk to wet sawdust.

<Okay, keep going that direction,> I told the Hork-Bajir.

Thought-speak is kind of like E-mail. You can address it to everyone, or you can address it to a

certain person. It sounds complicated, but you get used to it.

<Do you have a plan?> Rachel asked me so that the Hork-Bajir couldn't overhear.

<I hadn't really thought that far ahead,> I admitted.

<Do you know a safe place for them to hide?>

I searched my memory. I had to think like a human, not a bird. The Hork-Bajir couldn't exactly hide in trees.

<Yeah. There's a cave I know about. If we can keep them alive till then.>

The Hork-Bajir were running flat out. But now I saw a pair of big four-by-four pickup trucks coming from the other direction. The trucks raced along a dirt road, coming up to cut off the two fugitive Hork-Bajir. The Yeerks were pulling out all the stops.

<Man, this is like a really bad chess game where the other player has all the pieces,> I muttered.

<You *know* these woods, Tobias,> Rachel said. <That's our edge.>

<Yeah. We hope.> I turned my head left and right. Yes. I did know these woods. I knew where we were. I knew every tree and every ravine and every tiny stream.

<Okay, you guys, cut to your right now. There's a ditch. But there are a couple of Con-

trollers in your way. So you need to pass the big rock pile there, keeping it on your left.>

The Hork-Bajir hesitated, missed a couple of steps, and looked around in confusion.

<Did you guys hear me?>

<They heard you,> Rachel said tersely. <I think the instructions were too complicated.>

<Oh. Great. Oooookay. In that case, let's play follow the leader.> I took a deep breath and glanced around to make sure I knew exactly where I was. Then I spilled a little air from my wings, tried to keep all the speed I could, and dropped down into the trees. <Okay. Time to play "follow the big birdie"!>

I zoomed just over their heads.

<Yeah, me. The big brown bird with the pretty red tail. Follow me and stay close!>

<Tobias!> Rachel yelled. <One of the trucks is moving in ahead of you!>

I zoomed left and the twin monsters came racing right after me.

Have you ever flown at full speed right through a densely packed forest? Probably not. So let me tell you — it's exciting. Exciting like a video game set to the highest speed, where one wrong move means you're a bundle of crushed bird bones and feathers.

<Stay with me, boys, we're gonna be hauling butt,> I said. I shot between two trees that were

so close together I felt my wingtips brush rough bark. I cranked a right so sudden and sharp I almost splattered against an oak. And then I flapped hard to gain speed before the two not-very-bright Hork-Bajir ran over me.

High overhead, Rachel called down with up-dates.

<Tobias! Three dirt bikes on your left, con-verging!>

<Tobias, that truck is coming up behind you. They've spotted the Hork-Bajir!>

<Tobias! Look out! Guy with a gun!>

BOOM! BOOM!

Shotgun pellets ripped the air around me and stripped the leaves from a branch.

My flying muscles were aching, but I was too high on sheer adrenaline to care. It was insane! I was rocketing through the woods, barely missing tree trunks, just skimming above the saplings, blowing through territories belonging to other birds who'd have killed me themselves if I'd slowed down.

I was the rabbit and the two deadly Hork-Bajir were the dogs chasing me through the woods. And I'll say this for the Hork-Bajir — they may not be great at following instructions, but they knew how to stay on a target.

ZOOM! Through the trees!

ZOOM! Barely rising fast enough to clear a rocky outcropping!

ZOOM! Left!

ZOOM! Right!

ZOOM! Straight up with every single muscle screaming.

"Tseeeeeer!" I screamed in a combination of fear and total powered-up, red-tailed excitement.

Man, I was doing some serious flying.

But I was not getting close to my goal. And I was not losing the pursuing dirt bikes and four-by-fours.

<Tobias! Oh, man! There's a helicopter coming up from the south. Maybe two minutes away!>

<We're dead meat if that chopper gets here before we lose these Controllers on the ground. There's a stream. Think these monsters swim?>

<They don't look like they do,> Rachel said.

<Hork-Bajir. Can you swim? If you can, signal me by quickly slicing down the next sapling you come to.>

Slash! A sapling was suddenly shorter.

<All right then, stay with me!>

CHAPTER 7

I hung a brutally hard right and scraped my belly across a branch doing it. I fought my way through the grasping twigs and leaves and motored on.

<Thank goodness I ate a good breakfast,> I muttered.

<Tobias! You can't go that way. The trucks will cut you off! They have guys in the back of each one with shotguns.>

<No choice,> I said. <In about two minutes I'm going to collapse. And right about then that helicopter will get here!>

<Okay. Then we need to get rid of the guys with the guns,> Rachel said calmly. Like flying against a guy with a shotgun was no big deal.

<Rachel, have I ever mentioned that you are extremely cool?> I said. Then, to the Hork-Bajir: <Just keep running this same direction. Don't stop.>

I peeled away, and fought my way up and up and up, above the treetops. There was Rachel, gliding majestically on her huge eagle's wings. I needed altitude so I could turn it into speed.

Ahead, through the gaps in the tree cover, I could see the two pickup trucks. They were still bouncing along, kicking up dust as they hurried to cut off the Hork-Bajir.

In the back of each truck there was a man with a shotgun. These guys were holding on for dear life, so at least we had a chance of not getting killed.

<You take the one on the left. Ready?> I asked Rachel.

<Let's do it,> she said.

We aimed to intercept the trucks. Like a pair of cruise missiles, we targeted the spot where the trucks would be in five seconds. Four seconds. Three seconds.

I could see my guy clearly. Middle-aged human. He looked like a guy you'd see working in a hardware store or something. But he wasn't really human. The Yeerk in his head was aiming the gun.

Two seconds!

The Controller saw me. He frowned. Then he realized . . .

One second!

The shotgun came up. The twin barrels looked huge.

I raked my talons forward.

BOOM!

The shot passed millimeters over my head. I actually felt the wind!

"Tseeeeeer!"

I struck! The Controller fell off the back of the truck, clutching his face and howling.

A split second later, Rachel hit her target.

At that same instant the two Hork-Bajir came barreling out of the woods, right into the racing trucks. One jumped. He sailed over the truck and landed hard on the far side.

The second Hork-Bajir was too slow.

WHAM!

The truck slammed the Hork-Bajir. The Hork-Bajir went flying and sprawled in a brush-covered ditch.

BOOM! BOOM! Rachel's guy was firing blindly.

The first Hork-Bajir was up, but not running. I was close enough to hear him bellow in a voice full of despair.

"*Kalashi! Kalashi!*"

<Move, you idiot!> I screamed at the Hork-Bajir.

The two trucks had braked in a cloud of dust and dirt, fishtailing wildly on the narrow dirt road. Guys were piling out of the cabs, armed to the teeth.

From the edge of the woods, just down the road, three dirt bikes roared into sight.

BOOM! BOOM!

BLAMBLAMBLAM!

The Hork-Bajir froze. He looked up at me as I shot past him. And he said, "No! My *kalashi*! My wife!"

<Wife?> I said.

<Wife?> Rachel echoed.

That may have been the last word I'd ever expected to hear a Hork-Bajir say.

<You'll be dead in two seconds,> I snapped at the Hork-Bajir after I'd recovered from the shock. <Run. Run, or you're no good to anyone!>

He ran.

I guided him to the stream that lay half-concealed behind a stand of trees. He hit the water with surprisingly little splash and disappeared beneath the surface.

<He said *wife*, right?> I asked Rachel.

<Wife,> she agreed.

CHAPTER 8

"Wife? Excuse me, you said *wife*?" Marco asked incredulously. "You mean there's such a thing as a female Hork-Bajir?!"

<I guess so,> I said. <We didn't really have time to ask.>

It was late afternoon. We were all in Cassie's barn. Actually, I was in the rafters of Cassie's barn, looking down at the rest of the group — Jake, Cassie, Marco, Ax, and Rachel, back in human form again.

Ax was in his own, natural Andalite body. It's a danger to have him there because we can never allow anyone to see the Ax-man. I mean, one look at Aximili-Esgarrouth-Isthill, at the two movable stalk eyes on top of his head and the deadly scor-

36

pion tail and the centaur body, and you know he's not exactly a local boy.

But it was worth the risk, since he knew more about Hork-Bajir than any of us did. Besides, I was providing security. From my place up in the rafters, I could see out through the hayloft to Cassie's house. And since I have excellent hearing as well as sight, I'd know if anyone approached the barn.

Cassie's barn is actually the Wildlife Rehabilitation Clinic. It is full of every kind of local wild animal. The wire cages are piled high all around the barn.

Both Cassie's parents are veterinarians. Her mom works at The Gardens, which is this big amusement park and zoo complex.

Her father runs the clinic with a lot of help from Cassie. They take in injured or sick wild animals. And right now, beneath me in the cages, there was a sampling of all the animals that lived in the area — opossums, voles, rabbits, skunks, foxes, raccoons, squirrels, and so on. Many of them would have made a nice snack for me, but Cassie and I have an agreement about that — I don't eat her patients.

In addition to the land animals, there were bats and birds. Cassie actually rescues pigeons and crows and even jays. I have nothing against pigeons, but I don't like crows and ravens and

jays. They're like the gangsters of the bird world. Plus, they're smart. They can work together to mob peaceful raptors like me. Sometimes a bunch of them will actually try to steal a kill from me.

And believe me, you get six or eight big, fat jays or crows attacking you all at once, and it can be very annoying. But that's another story.

"How exactly do you tell a man Hork-Bajir from a woman Hork-Bajir?" Marco asked. "Do the women put makeup on their wrist blades? Do they use nail polish on those big nasty toes of theirs?"

Rachel rolled her eyes. "We didn't have a chance to go into it, all right? We barely got the one Hork-Bajir to the cave."

"I mean, do female Hork-Bajir cry at 'chick' movies?" Marco went on, talking mostly to himself. "Do they get all goo-goo when they see a baby?"

"What about the female?" Jake asked Rachel and me.

Rachel shrugged and looked away.

<We don't know,> I said. <We saw her get knocked into the ditch. That was it.>

"Man, this whole thing stinks. It's a trap. It's a setup," Marco said. "But I think the real question is, do female Hork-Bajir get all weird around bugs and snakes?"

<I don't think so. About the trap, I mean.>

"Weird around bugs and snakes?" Cassie asked with a raised eyebrow. "Is that how girls are, Marco?" With that, she reached into a low drawer beneath the bottom row of cages. A second later, a snake was lightly tossed through the air in Marco's direction.

"Ahhh! Ahhhh! Ahhhh! Get it off me!"

Cassie retrieved the harmless garden snake and put it back in its drawer while everyone laughed. Except Ax, who doesn't always get human humor.

Even Marco had to laugh. "Oh, that was so *not* fair. Funny, yes. Fair, no. Can we please act more mature here?"

"Sure, Marco," Rachel said. "Why don't you leave and we'll automatically be a more mature group?"

"Could we stick to business?" Jake asked. But he was still smiling from the snake thing, so no one took him too seriously.

"Why would a Yeerk . . . even a Yeerk inside a Hork-Bajir, want to run away?" Marco asked. "Sooner or later he has to get back to the Yeerk pool. It doesn't make any sense."

Rachel sighed. "Marco, how dumb are you? Don't you get it? These *aren't* Controllers. There is no Yeerk. Somehow these two Hork-Bajir are free."

Cassie looked thoughtful. "Isn't it kind of a

39

coincidence that you just happened to be in the area where the Hork-Bajir were escaping?"

<Yes,> I said. <Definitely. Especially since I wasn't even heading there. I was actually trying to go somewhere else.>

I saw the two stalk eyes on Ax's head swing up to focus on me with new interest. His main eyes stayed on Jake.

Cassie gave me a tilted-head puzzled look. "You mean —"

But Rachel interrupted. "Look, we need to decide what to do about this. We've got this Hork-Bajir male in a cave. But the Yeerks will keep looking for him. And I have to tell you, this Hork-Bajir is not exactly Stephen Hawking."

"Who?" Cassie asked.

<He is a human physicist,> Ax responded. <I've read some of his writings. He is very brilliant, but also very wrong about several things. For example, when he refers to the structure of atoms in —>

Jake threw up his hands in exasperation. "Is there *any* chance we could stick to business?"

"I remember when Jake used to be fun," Marco said in a loud whisper. "Now he's such a grown-up."

"I was *never* fun," Jake said with a tolerant smile.

"No, you were never *smart*, but you were *always* fun," Marco teased.

"The question is, what do we do about this Hork-Bajir?" Rachel asked. "He's sitting out there in a cave in the woods moaning about his *kalashi*. What do we do with him?"

We all looked at Ax like he'd have the answer.

<I have never known of a free Hork-Bajir,> Ax said. <They've been slaves of the Yeerks for a long time. But it is possible. Maybe somehow, while this Hork-Bajir's Yeerk was in the Yeerk pool, the Hork-Bajir managed to escape. It is possible. His wife as well. In which case these may be the only free Hork-Bajir in the entire galaxy. The only two free members of their species.>

"Imagine . . ." Cassie whispered. "Imagine being the only two free humans in all the world . . ."

Somehow no one felt like messing around anymore. Even Marco looked thoughtful. If the Yeerks won, humans would be no different than the Hork-Bajir — absolute slaves of the Yeerk empire.

"So what do we do with the only free Hork-Bajir in the galaxy?" Marco asked.

<What does the Hork-Bajir want to do?> Ax asked me and Rachel.

Rachel and I stared blankly at each other. <You know,> I admitted, <we never asked.>

"Then I guess that's step one," Jake said. "Let's find out what the Hork-Bajir wants."

Everyone agreed. But I saw that Cassie was still troubled. Under her breath she muttered, "And then let's find out why Tobias was somewhere he didn't mean to be."

I don't think anyone else heard her. But I did. Why *had* I been there?

CHAPTER 9

It took a while to figure out how we were going to deal with the Hork-Bajir. In the end, we decided I'd go ahead with Ax. The others would morph and stay close enough to hear what was happening.

The problem was, we were afraid to be honest with the Hork-Bajir. It could all still be some kind of a trap. We couldn't let anyone know who we really were. Or *what* we really were.

See, the Yeerks know that there is someone out here messing with them. They know they're being attacked by someone using animal morphs. Since only the Andalites have the power to morph, the Yeerks assume we must all be An-

dalites. They figure we must be a group of An-dalite guerillas.

We want them to think that. We sure don't want them realizing that the Animorphs are mostly a bunch of human kids. If they ever found out where Jake and Cassie and Rachel and Marco live . . . well, that would be the end of us.

The cave where Rachel and I left the Hork-Bajir was small for a creature of his size. It was hidden by brush and fallen branches. It went in about twenty feet, but was only about five feet tall.

I landed on a fallen branch outside the cave entrance. I waited till everyone was in posi-tion. Then I said, <Hey, in there. Hork-Bajir. It's me, the talking bird. I'm coming in. With a friend.>

It's hard for a bird to push through bushes and thorns, so Ax stepped forward, almost dainty on his four hooves. He pushed the tangle aside with his weak arms. He stuck his head inside the dark cave.

The reaction was immediate.

"*Hruthin!* Andalite!"

A bladed arm slashed, missing Ax's head by inches. Ax jerked back and cocked his tail to strike.

<NO!> I yelled. <Listen in there, you weed-

whacker-looking jerk, calm down! And Ax-man, take it easy!>

The bladed arm withdrew slowly, and Ax relaxed his tail.

I took a few seconds to slow my heart down. When a bird is startled it wants to fly. Natural instinct. I had to fight to control it and stay put.

<What's going on?> Cassie asked.

I looked up at the sky. Rachel and Cassie were up there in bird morph, Rachel as her bald-eagle self and Cassie as an owl. The sun was just setting. And when darkness fell an owl would be a lot more useful than an eagle. The two of them were flying cover. Making sure we weren't disturbed.

<Oh, nothing much,> I said. <We're all just saying hello. By the way, is everything clear up there, Cassie? Rachel?>

<Yep. Everything is clear,> Rachel called down.

I took a couple of deep breaths and tried to steady my nerves. Neither Ax nor I wanted to go into that cave anymore. You just can't be careless when you're dealing with Hork-Bajir. One fast move and they can leave you wondering why your head is rolling across the grass.

<Hork-Bajir, come on out,> I said firmly.

Slowly the big creature crawled out. He stood erect, blinking in the dim evening light.

"Not *Hork-Bajir*," he said. "Jara Hamee. My name. Jara Hamee."

<He's kidding, right?> Jake said in my head. <His name is Jeremy?>

I glanced up to see a big, round, white-and-orange face. A face with deep, intelligent eyes and yellowish teeth about four inches long. It was Jake, in his tiger morph. He was above the cave opening on an outcropping of rock. If the Hork-Bajir had made a wrong move, Jake would have been all over him.

<You better talk to our boy Jara Hamee here,> I said to Ax. I figured Ax would know more about talking to other aliens than me.

Ax held his hands open in a gesture of peace. He lowered his tail still further. I could see he really didn't want to do that. The air between the Andalite and the Hork-Bajir seemed to crackle with tension.

<My name is Aximili,> Ax said.

"You are *Hruthin*. Andalite."

<Yes.>

"You kill me?"

<No. I won't kill you,> Ax said.

"*Hruthin* kill Hork-Bajir," the Hork-Bajir named Jara Hamee said. "Hork-Bajir kill *Hruthin*."

<This is going really well,> Marco said dryly. Then he sang new words for that *Barney* song. <I kill you, you kill me, we're an alien family . . .>

46

I saw Marco settling in behind a stand of trees off to the left. He looked like a very large, very hairy man. A gorilla, actually. We had decided to have plenty of muscle ready, just in case the Hork-Bajir turned out to be trouble.

<Andalites tried to save the Hork-Bajir from the Yeerks,> Ax said, sounding a little defensive.

The Hork-Bajir stared at Ax's face. "You *darkap*. You fail."

<Yes. We failed. But I'm here now. And I don't kill Hork-Bajir . . . unless they are tools of the Yeerks.>

The Hork-Bajir made a sort of forward jerk with its head and a raspy little sound in its throat. It sounded like a derisive laugh. But who knows? I had no idea what a Hork-Bajir laugh should sound like. Or even if they laughed at all.

WHAP!

The Hork-Bajir slapped his chest with his left hand. It startled me enough that I was halfway airborne before I got a grip.

The Hork-Bajir threw out his arm and said, "Jara Hamee escaped the Yeerks. Jara Hamee free! Jara Hamee has his own head." He pressed both hands gently against his snakelike head.

<How do we *know* you are free? How do we know you "have your own head"?> Ax asked him coldly.

The Hork-Bajir looked puzzled. Then, to my complete and total shock, he made a quick movement of his arm.

It was faster than a human eye could have seen.

But I saw it.

I saw the wrist blade slice right into his own head. *He sliced right into his own head!*

<No!> I yelled in horror.

<Yah!> Jake yelped.

There was a gash six inches deep in the Hork-Bajir's head. He reached up with his clawed hands and pulled the gash open. He pulled his own head open! And it's not like it didn't hurt him. I could see the pain on his face.

Blood — or something — oozed in shades of deep red and deeper blue-green. He held the gash open and we stared, Ax and me, right into the Hork-Bajir's brain. I guess Jake and Marco could see it pretty clearly, too.

<Oh, man,> Marco moaned. <Can I just say "yuck"?>

Jara Hamee pressed the two sides of the gash together. He held the cut for a few seconds, and with amazing speed, the bleeding coagulated.

A long scab began to form over the gash.

That's when I started breathing again. I had stopped. Then I started my heart up. I swear it had stopped, too.

<Did you see a Yeerk in there in his head?> I asked Ax shakily.

<No,> Ax said, just as shaken as I was. <No Yeerk.>

<Did that scare the pee out of you, Ax-man, or doesn't that kind of thing bother you Andalites?>

<I am as peeless as you, Tobias, my friend.>

<That wasn't necessary,> I told Jara Hamee.

His face — insofar as he had a face — was still scrunched up in pain. He was breathing hard and sweating the same blue-green fluid I'd seen inside his head.

"Necessary," he grunted through his pain. "Jara Hamee is strong. But Jara Hamee needs help."

<Help to do what?> Ax asked him gently.

The Hork-Bajir stared at Ax, then shifted his gaze to me. "Flying animal saw my *kalashi*. Jara Hamee must find her. Jara Hamee . . ." He struggled to come up with a word. Then he made a gesture with his hands, as if someone were tearing something out of him. As if someone were removing his heart.

There was no question what it meant. Even across the huge divide between our species, I could recognize that emotion.

<You love her,> I said.

"Jara Hamee loves," the Hork-Bajir said. "*Kalashi*, Jara Hamee free. Want free."

Ax swiveled his stalk eyes back toward me. <I think I believe him.>

<Yeah. Me, too, Ax.>

<Hey. You guys down there?> Cassie called down from above. <We have company coming.>

CHAPTER 10

<Ш hat kind of company, Cassie?> I heard Jake snap.

<Fifteen, maybe twenty people. They're strung out in a line. Coming this way.>

<And I have an equal number coming from the southeast,> Rachel said. <And . . . oh, man. They have Hork-Bajir with them! It's not even dark and they're bringing Hork-Bajir out! In the open!>

<They want our boy here real badly,> I said. <It's a big risk running aliens through the woods when it's still light enough to see.>

<They're converging on you,> Cassie reported. <I have a small troop of Hork-Bajir coming up, too. Oh, man. This isn't good. You guys

51

are practically surrounded. You have maybe five minutes till they're all over you.>

<Talk about bad timing. It's getting late,> Marco pointed out. <It's almost dinnertime. My dad will give me much grief if I don't get home in time for dinner.>

Jake laughed. So did I. It was just so ridiculous having to worry about being grounded when we were halfway surrounded by Yeerks.

<We could easily escape,> Ax said. <We can all morph some small animal or bird and not be seen.>

<That wouldn't help old Jara Hamee here,> Marco said.

<Distraction,> Jake said. <We need to draw the bad guys away.>

<But the Yeerks are looking for a Hork-Bajir,> Ax pointed out. <Will they be foolish enough to follow any of us?>

<We can only hope they will,> Jake said tersely. <We can get away, but I don't think we can leave Jara Hamee behind.>

But I had a different idea. Unfortunately, it was a dangerous idea. A very dangerous idea. And the danger would all be on someone else. Not me.

I hesitated. It makes me sick when other people take risks that I can't take. <Look, uh . . . there might be a way . . .> I said at last.

<What?> Jake asked.

<They want a Hork-Bajir to chase, right? Well, we could give them one.>

<Morph a Hork-Bajir?> Marco asked. <Ewwww.>

<Jara Hamee isn't just any animal,> Cassie objected. <He's sentient. He's self-aware.>

<Ax morphed me once,> Jake pointed out. <And Cassie, you morphed Rachel.>

<I'm just saying we have to get Jara Hamee's permission, at least,> Cassie said. <But whatever you decide, do it quick!>

<I'll do it. I'll morph the Hork-Bajir,> Rachel said. Suddenly I saw her glide down through the trees on her huge eagle wings. <I need to change morphs, anyway. It's getting too dark for eagle eyes.>

<No. I should do it,> Ax said quickly.

<No way,> Rachel said. She was already starting to demorph. <I have dibs.>

<Dibs?>

<I spoke first,> Rachel explained.

Ax let it go and focused his main eyes back on the Hork-Bajir. <Yeerks are coming. One of my friends wishes to morph you. To trick the Yeerks. Do you agree?>

"Jara Hamee hates Yeerks," the big Hork-Bajir said. Like that was all the answer he needed to give.

<Okay then, turn around, Jara Hamee,> I ordered the Hork-Bajir. <Close your eyes and don't look till I tell you. If you open your eyes this *Hruthin* here . . . this Andalite . . . will slice and dice you. You got it? Eyes closed.>

The Hork-Bajir turned around obediently. I would have laughed if I wasn't feeling half-sick with worry for Rachel. I mean, this seven-foot-tall monster was taking orders from a twenty-inch-long bird.

But my sense of humor was slightly damaged right then. Rachel was going to morph a Hork-Bajir. And then she was going to draw off the Yeerks. She was going to make them chase her.

It made me sick to think about it. It had been my idea. My brilliant idea. And *she* would take the risk.

Rachel began to emerge from her eagle body. She rose up swiftly from the pine needle and rotting leaf floor of the forest. Up and up, a weird, misshapen, nightmare creature made of fair human flesh and dark brown feathers, bright yellow beak, and lengthening legs.

I would have given anything to be able to go in her place. But I can't morph. I would be safe in the sky or in the trees while she was trying to outrun the enemy.

It was the story of my life lately. My friends

went into danger, and I stayed safe. All because I couldn't morph.

In a minute Rachel was no longer a bird, but a human girl. A human girl who even now, even with all of us scared, managed to look like some smiling magazine cover girl.

<You don't have to do this, Rachel,> I said.

<It's Rachel's greatest thrill,> Marco said. <Morph a Hork-Bajir? Hey, she'll finally get to become on the *outside* what she's always been *inside*.>

<Shut up, Marco,> I snapped.

Rachel gave me a look that said, "Don't worry, Tobias." But she said nothing because she was now fully human. We still didn't want the Hork-Bajir to know we were human. We didn't want him to hear a human voice.

The Hork-Bajir stood peacefully as Rachel reached out her slender fingers to touch the creature's back. The Hork-Bajir went slightly limp as she began to "acquire" him. To absorb his DNA and make it part of her.

<Guys?> Cassie called down from the sky. <I'm serious now. The bad guys are definitely getting close. I can see them.>

With my hawk's hearing, I heard the sounds of heavy creatures stomping and crashing clumsily through the woods. I heard the metallic clank

of weapons against belts and the muttered commands between human-Controllers and Hork-Bajir.

<Cassie's right,> I said. <We're down to two minutes maximum.>

Rachel gave a nod. She sent me a cocky wink. She closed her eyes and focused on the new morph.

And then . . . Rachel began to change. I wanted to turn away, but somehow I felt like I owed it to her to watch. It was because of me this was happening to her.

I can't tell you how utterly bizarre that scene was. The woods were growing dark. Shadows were deep all around, and even with my hawk's eyes I couldn't see through the shadows. Overhead the sky was dark blue streaked with red and orange, not yet black. True night was still an hour away. But under the shade of the trees it was night already.

We stood there, an insane nightmare of creatures — the Hork-Bajir, eyes closed tight; the Andalite, deadly tail twitching nervously at the prospect of battle; the orange-and-black-striped tiger climbing down from the rocks, moving like liquid power; a gorilla walking erect, using its massive fists as extra feet; and me . . . the Bird-boy.

And in the middle of our group was Rachel.

She was growing taller now. She was already tall for a girl, but now she was quickly heading toward Shaq-size.

Her skin was changing. It turned dark, almost green-black. Her feet mutated swiftly from dainty human to the three-toed, one-spur feet of the Hork-Bajir. Feet that looked like my own talons except much, much larger.

Her face grew elongated. The jaw bulged outward and became smooth as a bullet. Her eyes were narrow, red-tinged slits. And then the blades began to appear.

SHWOOP! Horn-blades exploded from her forehead!

SHWOOP! Blades appeared at the wrists and elbows!

SHWOOP! Blades grew at her knees!

Rachel had become a walking razor. Seven feet of muscled deadly speed.

<So,> Rachel said. <So this is a Hork-Bajir.>

CHAPTER 11

<You can open your eyes now,> I told Jara Hamee.

He did. And he turned to face . . . himself. Rachel was an identical copy of the Hork-Bajir, grown from his own DNA. I don't know what I expected. But it sure wasn't what happened next.

"HeeeeRRRROOOOOWW!" Rachel bellowed in a voice that made the leaves quake.

"HeeeeRRRROOOOWWW-Unh!" Jara Hamee responded.

<Shut up, you idiots!> Marco cried frantically. <We're halfway surrounded by Yeerks!>

SSSSEEEWW! Rachel slashed viciously at

58

the air! She missed Jara Hamee by an inch! Half an inch!

Jara Hamee responded instantly with a forward stab of one of his big feet. If it had connected, it would have ripped Rachel's stomach open. But the blow missed by a hair.

Rachel slashed and Jara Hamee slashed, but all the blows missed. Not by much, but they did miss.

<Back off!> Jake yelled. <Stop it!> I could see he was getting ready to jump in between them. That was all we needed — a three-way fight between two Hork-Bajir and a tiger.

<Jake, wait! I think . . . I think it's just a ritual,> I said. <You see this kind of thing all the time in nature. It's a dominance ritual.>

The two Hork-Bajir had stopped slashing. Now they preened, circling around each other, stretching up on tiptoes to see who was taller.

<Hey, we so totally do *not* have time for games,> Marco said.

He was right. I saw flashlights through the trees.

Jara Hamee and Rachel bent their heads forward and touched their scythelike horns together with surprising gentleness.

<Rachel, are you okay in there?> I asked her.

<What? Um . . . what?> she asked. She was

confused. Morphing a new creature is confusing. Sometimes the experience can be overwhelming. The instincts of the creature surface and can even take over control for a while.

Or that's what everyone tells me, anyway. It's been a while since I morphed.

<Rachel? We are out of time,> Jake said gently. <Are you up for this?>

<Um . . . yeah. Uh . . . okay. Sure. Sorry. I got kind of caught up there for a minute. I'm not getting Jara Hamee's thoughts or memories, but I definitely got a big bundle of Hork-Bajir instincts.>

<Jara Hamee? Back in the cave,> Jake said. <Do not come out. Everyone get ready. We just want to lead the Yeerks away. We are not looking for a fight. Rachel? You hear that about not looking for a fight?>

<Mmm-hmm. Sure,> Rachel said, even as she slashed at the air, trying out the Hork-Bajir blades. <Whatever.>

<Rachel, you can still back out of this,> I suggested.

<I'll bet you ten bucks she says, "Let's do it,"> Marco said quickly.

Rachel turned her snakelike head toward Marco and grinned what I think was a Hork-Bajir grin. <Let's . . . go for it.>

<Oh, man!> Marco complained. <She cheated.>

And then the enemy arrived. Suddenly four human-Controllers armed with guns crashed clumsily into view. And with them, two Hork-Bajir.

They saw Jake and Rachel and me.

They did not see Marco. He lumbered up behind one of the Hork-Bajir, tapped him on the shoulder, and the instant the Hork-Bajir turned, Marco landed a punch that would have split a telephone pole.

Ka-BOOM!

The Hork-Bajir went down hard.

"Whoa!" one of the humans cried.

And suddenly the Controllers weren't chasing us. We were chasing them.

I flapped hard and landed on Rachel's forward-swept horn blade. I gripped the bone blade with my talons.

<What are you doing?> Rachel asked.

<Just hitching a ride,> I said. <I'm not going to be left out. Not this time.>

<Cool. Let's go.>

<Yee-hah!> I yelled with totally, *totally* fake enthusiasm.

We took off through the woods. Rachel's Hork-Bajir body had an easy, loping run that was faster than it seemed at first.

I sat there holding on tight. I was tense and scared and ready for trouble. But at least I was in for the fight, you know? At least I wasn't off somewhere safe while the others ran all the risks.

<You guys!> Cassie called down from above. <Stop chasing those Controllers! They're setting up a trap. They're leading you right between two bunches of bad guys!>

<Oops. Time to turn around,> I told Rachel.

<Yep.>

She turned and started running in a new direction. She was like some big tank, and I was the hood ornament.

Then . . .

<Yaaahhh!> Rachel cried. She pitched forward. I pitched forward. We hit the ground hard, and rolled through a juniper bush.

<Sorry. I tripped. You okay, Tobias?>

<Yeah. I think so.>

I was caught in the branches of the bush. I couldn't fight too hard to get out or I'd damage my feathers.

Slice!

Slice!

Suddenly the juniper branches were gone.

<All right! I like these blades,> Rachel said. <Excellent!>

I fluttered my wings and hopped up to get back on Rachel's horns. But I must have overshot my goal because suddenly I was flying through the air.

No, wait! Hold on! I was up above the trees! Impossible!

How did I get here? I hadn't even flown. I'd barely hopped and now I was up in the sky? What the . . . ?

I did a quick turnaround, trying to figure out where I was. The sun was setting fast and there wasn't enough light for me to use my full powers of sight. But I wasn't blind, either. I saw a horned owl floating just at treetop level. Cassie. But she was so far away. Maybe a quarter mile!

<No way,> I said in total confusion.

Then I heard gunfire. Quite close. In fact, just beneath me.

BLAM! BLAM!

A human voice yelled, "Freeze! Freeze or I put the next shot in your second heart."

There was a small clearing below me. I knew the meadow. It was the territory of a Swainson's hawk. Not as nice as my own meadow, but a nice territory, anyway.

But I wasn't looking for mice in this clearing. I saw three humans, each well-armed, surrounding a single Hork-Bajir.

Rachel?

No. Couldn't be. She was back . . . back where I *should* be. Was it Jara Hamee himself? What was going on?

I noticed that one of the human-Controllers

63

seemed to be sick. He was doubling over, like he was having a spasm. No, wait! He was morphing!

It took a few seconds for me to be sure. But when I saw the extra stalk eyes appear and the sharp-tipped tail, I knew. It was an Andalite.

There are only two Andalites on planet Earth. One is Ax. The other is not a true Andalite at all. It's a Yeerk who uses an Andalite body.

The only Andalite-Controller in all the galaxy. The only Yeerk to have the power to morph.

Our greatest enemy, leader of the Yeerk invasion of Earth, murderer of Ax's brother, Elfangor.

Visser Three.

CHAPTER 12

Andalites always look like they're right on the borderline between cute and dangerous. But with Visser Three, that line doesn't even exist.

It's not that he looks any different *outside*. I mean, he looks like an older Andalite is all. But there is some dark, evil glow that shines from within him. And when you meet him you have no doubt . . . no doubt at all that he is dangerous.

Deadly dangerous.

<Guys?> I called in thought-speak. <Um, Jake? Rachel?>

No answer. I was too far away from them.

The Andalite body emerged fully from the human form it had morphed.

<Well, well, Ket Halpak,> Visser Three said.

<That is your name, isn't it? Your original Hork-Bajir name? You've run us a nice chase, but it's time to come home now.>

Visser Three seldom bothered to whisper his thought-speak. I guess when you're that powerful it never occurs to you to worry that someone might overhear.

Ket Halpak, he had called the Hork-Bajir. So it was not Jara Hamee. This was his *kalashi*. His wife.

They had her surrounded. Two humans carrying shotguns and Visser Three, armed with all the lightning speed of an Andalite. Not to mention morphs from all the dark corners of the galaxy.

There was no way to save the Hork-Bajir female. I'd have to take Visser Three out, and that wasn't going to happen. See, Andalites — even false Andalites — are impossible to sneak up on.

Those extra stalk eyes, turning this way and that, always looking in every direction, made it impossible.

Unless . . .

Unless there was a distraction. I knew the Swainson's hawk tended to roost in one particular elm tree. The light was too dim to see him. He might not even be there. But if he was . . .

I flapped hard to gain altitude. Not too much, there wasn't time. Just enough. Forty feet. Fifty feet. Sixty feet. Then . . . I folded my wings and plummeted toward the ground.

"Tseeeeeeeeer!" I screamed in the voice of a red-tail.

"Tseeeeeeeeer!" I called again, making sure the Swainson's hawk would hear me.

And down I came, wings back and tail narrowed for maximum speed. I aimed straight for Visser Three.

If the Swainson's hawk wasn't home, I was toast.

Then, a rustling sound from the elm! From the corner of my eye I saw wings flapping. The Swainson's was coming out to defend his territory against the pushy red-tail.

I've never been so relieved to see a fellow hawk.

<That bird! It's probably one of them!> Visser Three shouted, pointing at the Swainson's.

The two human-Controllers spun and raised their shotguns to their shoulders. And Visser Three, bless his evil heart, turned his stalk eyes toward what he thought was a threat.

<I'm a friend of Jara Hamee,> I said to the Hork-Bajir. <Get ready!>

Talons forward! Beak thrust out! A sudden flaring of wings to adjust the angle and . . .

Strike!

My talons raked Visser Three's exposed stalk eyes from behind.

<ARRRRRHHHH!> Visser Three bellowed in pain.

<Now, RUN!> I told the Hork-Bajir.

BLAM! BLAM! BLAM! The shotguns fired.

And we were out of there! Out! Of! There!

The Hork-Bajir bolted. I flapped like my life depended on it. It did.

The Swainson's hawk turned so hard, so fast, I thought he'd been hit. But then he was hauling his tail feathers outta there, too.

<Andalite filth!> I heard Visser Three scream in my head.

But by then I was out over the trees and the Hork-Bajir was running flat-out below me, and I was just screaming like an idiot from the sheer insane rush of it all.

<Yesss! Yesss! Bird-boy shoots, he scores! Yah-HAH!>

CHAPTER 13

Jara Hamee and Ket Halpak were reunited in the shelter of the cave.

We were all exhausted and scared and confused. But we also had that slightly lunatic rush that comes from cheating death.

Marco and Cassie were both fretting about being late getting home. And everyone was getting close to the two-hour morphing limit. But despite all that, it was kind of sweet seeing the two Hork-Bajir together.

They didn't exactly hug. I guess hugging doesn't work all that well when you have blades all over. Ket Halpak did touch the healing wound Jara Hamee had made in his own head.

<Look, we have to get out of here,> Rachel

69

said. She was still in her Hork-Bajir form. <I'll be grounded for the weekend if I don't get home. And I have the feeling we're going to be busy this weekend, so I can't get grounded.>

<Your mom wouldn't ground a Packard Foundation Outstanding Student, would she?> I asked.

There was a kind of embarrassed silence. I wasn't supposed to know about Rachel's award.

<It's not that big a deal,> Rachel said. She looked down at the ground.

<What do we do about these guys?> Jake asked. He was still in tiger morph. There were scratches and cuts on his sinuous orange-and-black fur. While I was off rescuing Ket Halpak, there had been a skirmish between the rest of my friends and some Controllers.

No one had been hurt. But once again, I wasn't there when the real fighting started.

<You guys go on home,> I told the others. <I'll keep watch over our Hork-Bajir friends here.>

<You can't keep watch all night,> Rachel protested.

<Hey, I have nothing else to do. I'll take a perch in the tree by the cave entrance. Not a problem.>

<I will help keep watch, too,> Ax chimed in.

<Let's, um, go outside and talk about this,>

Jake said. To the Hork-Bajir he said, <Jara and Ket? You have to stay in this cave till we come and get you. Tomorrow some time.>

"What will you do with Ket Halpak and Jara Hamee?" Jara asked.

<We really don't know yet,> Jake answered honestly.

"We will wait. Here."

"We *fellana* . . . we thank you," Ket said.

Outside it had definitely turned dark now. No stars in the sky yet, but it was just a matter of minutes. Everyone demorphed while Ax and I kept a nervous watch.

"Okay, so what do we do about this?" Jake asked, once everyone but me was normal again.

I kept pace with the others by flitting from branch to branch. I'd let them walk a little way ahead, then fly a few yards ahead of them and wait till they caught up.

"We have two real live aliens," Rachel said. "We could take them to the media. How can you deny there is a Yeerk conspiracy when you see those two?"

<There is already a real, live alien among you,> Ax pointed out. <Me. But I have learned about human society. Humans invent all sorts of things that are not true. I have seen photographs of aliens in human newspapers. Do most people believe them?>

"Those aren't *real* newspapers," Marco said. "No one with half a brain believes those supermarket tabloids."

"And how do we know which newspapers and which TV networks are already infiltrated by the Yeerks?" Cassie said. "We could end up handing the Hork-Bajir right back to the Yeerks."

"Well, what exactly are we supposed to do with Romeo and Juliet back there?" Marco asked sarcastically. "Rent them an apartment? Buy them a house? Get them jobs? I mean, they are just *slightly* obvious. You know? People are probably going to notice them if they start shopping at the mall."

We all laughed. But it was a brief laugh. The truth is, we didn't know what to do.

<Those two may be the only free Hork-Bajir in all the galaxy,> Ax said. <The only two free Hork-Bajir in existence.>

"Like members of an endangered species," Cassie said thoughtfully. "The last two free Hork-Bajir. Maybe the last hope of their kind."

"Oh, man," Marco groaned. "Cassie, don't start in with the ecology stuff, okay? Those are not a pair of spotted owls or humpback whales back there."

<I must stop here,> Ax said. <We are close to the edge of the forest.>

Everyone stopped. Even though they all were

real anxious to get home to be yelled at by their various parents, no one left.

"What Cassie said may be true," Jake pointed out. "These two are an endangered species. What do you do with an endangered species?"

Cassie shrugged. "You find them a safe, protected environment. And then you hope they have lots of little Hork-Bajir, and somehow the species survives."

"Um, hello. This is *Earth*," Marco said. "There is no safe place for an alien that looks like a mix of gargoyle and a lawn mower."

<Yes, there is,> I said.

Four human heads and one Andalite set of eyes all turned to stare up at me.

"Where?" Rachel asked.

<I know a place. Way up in the mountains. A valley. There are caves and fresh water streams. It's hidden.>

The picture of the place was clear in my mind. I could see it perfectly. I saw a beautiful waterfall. I saw tall trees that practically blotted out the sky in some areas. And a wide meadow filled with wildflowers. In my mind I could even imagine the place being home to Hork-Bajir.

<Maybe we could take them there,> I suggested.

Jake shrugged. "We don't have any better plan. Right?"

"Right now I need to think about what story I'm going to tell my dad when I get home," Marco said. "Tomorrow we can worry about taking Adam and Eve Hork-Bajir off to Tobias's Garden of Eden."

Not a bad description, I thought. That was a little what the valley was like. I could see the place as clearly in my mind as any place I had ever been.

There was just one little problem. I'd never been there. I'd never actually seen it.

And I had no idea where the lovely pictures in my mind had come from.

CHAPTER 14

I usually spent the night in my favorite nighttime perch. It's a high branch, up in the very middle of an incredibly old oak. I like the rough oak bark because it's easy to hold onto. I can sink my talons deep and drift off to my dreams.

My regular perch is deep within the tree because it keeps me out of sight of the night predators. The raccoons and foxes and wolves all work at night. They don't worry me too much. Wolves and foxes don't climb trees very well.

I do keep an eye out for raccoons because they can climb when they want to. And they are nasty, dangerous enemies. But it's a rare raccoon that can climb my tree without my hearing him.

I worry more about owls. Not that they usually prey on something as large and tough as a red-tailed hawk. Mostly they eat mice, same as I do. But they still scare me because they have powers I don't have.

I'm used to having this edge over all the other creatures. In the daylight I hear better than most animals, and I see better than any of them. My vision is many times better than human vision. If I were at home plate and you were holding a book open way out in right field, I'd be able to read it. If you were walking by on the other side of the street, I'd be able to see a flea crawling around in your hair. But that's all in daylight. At night I see a little better than a human . . . I mean, better than a normal human. But not much better.

That's why the owls scare me. They see through darkness like I see through daylight. To an owl I'm as visible as if I were outlined in bright red flashing neon. And an owl doesn't make any noise as it flies in for the kill. No noise. None.

It makes me nervous. But what can you do? I guess everyone has problems, right?

But at night as I listen for the sounds of raccoons scrabbling and open my eyes to watch the ghostly owls do their killing work, I wish I had a house.

If you asked me what I think of being a red-tailed hawk, I'd give you two different answers, depending on the time of day. When the sun is up, and the thermals are piling up the tall clouds, and I'm riding the high breezes a million miles above the humans who crawl along below me . . . well, then I'd say it's great.

But at night, when I cower on my branch and peer half-blind through the leaves at a cold moon and can only listen to the sounds of the night predators doing their work, well, that's different.

This particular night was different for a couple of reasons. I was not on my regular perch. I was in a scruffy pine tree that was located near the cave. I was standing guard over the Hork-Bajir, listening for any threats to them. I was out of my normal territory, in an unfamiliar tree. And I was jumpy.

As I sat there with my talons dug into bark, I heard the high-pitched squeal of a mouse.

I drifted back toward sleep. I tried to remember what it had been like to sleep in a bed at night. But I couldn't really remember. I could only imagine what it was like for the others.

Cassie, Jake, Marco, Rachel, all asleep in their beds. All with covers pulled up and pillows fluffed. Alarm clocks glowing on their night-stands.

I heard a sound. My eyes opened. I peered down through the branches and saw a shape like a deformed deer, ghostly pale in the filtered moonlight.

<Hi, Ax-man,> I said.

<Hello, Tobias. You heard me? I was trying to be silent.>

<You're very quiet. For a big old four-legged, two-handed, four-eyed, scorpion-tailed alien.>

Ax laughed. <One of these nights I may show you.>

<Hah. Right. And eagles may fly out of my butt.>

<Is that possible?> Ax asked, sounding alarmed.

<No. See, that's why it's funny.>

<I understand,> Ax said, clearly not understanding at all.

Nights in the forest have gotten a bit better since Ax joined our little group. Having him around is not exactly like being in a nice, snug bed. But it's good to have someone to talk to. The other forest animals don't have much to say.

<Our two Hork-Bajir are pretty quiet in there,> I told Ax. <They were talking earlier. Mostly in their own language. But even then they used some English words. Why is that?>

<The Hork-Bajir were never a very intellectual species,> Ax said, with a hint of snobbery. <Their own language was primitive. It only had about five hundred words. That's what we learned in

school, anyway. I suppose it's true. I guess for duty here on Earth, the Yeerks thought they should be able to speak a few words of a human language.>

<I didn't mean to eavesdrop on them,> I said. <But it was easy for me to hear. They kept using some Hork-Bajir word. It sounded like *kawatnoj*. Something like that, anyway.>

<I don't know the word,> Ax admitted. <I don't speak Hork-Bajir. I'll ask them tomorrow what it means.>

<Maybe you shouldn't. They don't seem to like you Andalites.>

<We tried to save them from the Yeerks,> Ax said with sudden anger. <We failed, yes. But we did try. Why should they hate us?>

<I don't know, Ax-man. Maybe they've had Yeerks in their heads for so long they've just absorbed the Yeerk hatred of Andalites.>

<Well. The Yeerks *should* hate us. We Andalites will defeat them in the end! And of course, you humans will help, too.>

I laughed silently. I like Ax, but he is a bit arrogant about his own species.

<I guess I'll go patrol around again,> Ax said. <I haven't seen or heard anything unusual, though. Do you really think we can lead these Hork-Bajir safely to this mountain valley you mentioned earlier?>

I didn't answer. Mentioning the valley just reminded me. <Ax? Have you ever just had information pop into your head and not know where it came from?>

<No. I don't think so. Maybe something I forgot and then remembered later.>

<No, this is like stuff I couldn't possibly know. It's like . . . > I froze.

Taxxons!

They were crawling through the woods. I could see them in my mind — huge centipedes, each as big around as a redwood tree. They moved on dozens of rows of needle-sharp legs. They held the upper third of their bodies erect, keeping their fragile rows of upper legs clear of the ground.

I could see them in my mind! I could see the gasping round mouths ringed with teeth. I could see the jelly-glob eyes.

<Tobias?> Ax asked, sounding concerned.

<Taxxons,> I said. <There are definitely Taxxons coming!>

<Where?> Ax asked in alarm. His tail cocked back, ready for a fight.

<I . . . they're coming. I . . .> I looked around me at the dark woods. No sign of anything strange. Let alone Taxxons. But I was dead sure they were coming, just the same.

<Ax? You know how I was just talking about

knowing things I couldn't possibly know? It just happened again. Just now. There are like a dozen Taxxons coming this way. Somehow they can smell the Hork-Bajir. Like bloodhounds.>

All four of Ax's eyes looked up at me. He looked grim. <Taxxon trackers can sense warm flesh from miles away, as long as they have a sample. They're a special breed of Taxxon. How did you know that? How did you know Taxxon trackers hunt by smell?>

<I don't know, Ax. But I am sure going to find out,> I said angrily. <Someone or something is using me, and I don't like it very much.>

Ax ignored my outburst. <If the Yeerks have sent Taxxons, they'll back them up with Hork-Bajir or humans. No amount of Taxxons could ever destroy a pair of Hork-Bajir. Jara Hamee and Ket Halpak could slice up Taxxons all day.>

<Can we throw the Taxxons off the scent?> I asked.

<No. If they have smelled these Hork-Bajir, nothing will throw them off.>

<Then we have to move the Hork-Bajir. Now. Taxxons can't be all that fast. But we need to move out. Ax? I can get the Hork-Bajir started. You have to get to Jake quickly. Tell him what's happening.>

<Yes, Tobias. I'll do that. But how will we find you if you're busy hiding from the Yeerks?>

<Take to the air. You all have bird of raptor morphs — eagles, ospreys, falcons. Use them. There's nothing raptor eyes can't find. I'll be heading toward the mountains.>

Heading toward the mountains with a pair of Hork-Bajir, while someone or something used me like a sock puppet.

Well, that was going to change. I was the predator. I was the hunter. No one was going to use me.

CHAPTER 15

<Jara Hamee, we have to go. Right now,> I told the Hork-Bajir as Ax ran off into the night.

Jara stuck his bladed snakelike head out through the bushes. "What has happened?"

<Taxxons are tracking you.>

I swear he went pale. His narrow eyes widened in fear. "Taxxon," he said, as if the very word made him want to spit.

But he reacted very quickly after that. He went back into the cave and came back out with Ket. I still couldn't really tell one of them from the other. At least not in the dark.

"Dark," Ket said, looking around.

<Yeah, I know. But I guess that won't stop the Taxxons. So let's get going.>

But how exactly we were supposed to move through the pitch-black forest, I had no idea. I couldn't see. And to my disappointment, the Hork-Bajir were not all that good at seeing in the dark, either.

It was tough going. I couldn't exactly drag my feathers through thorn bushes. The Hork-Bajir couldn't fly. And it was totally dark. The kind of dark you only get when you are a long way from the lights of homes and cars and streetlamps. It was so dark you couldn't see a tree till you ran into it. It was like being blind.

I rode on Jara Hamee's horns, just like I had with Rachel. Only we were moving more slowly and trying not to leave tracks.

"Where?" Jara Hamee asked. "Go where?"

<I don't really know,> I grumbled. <I guess the little voice in my head will tell me.>

The Hork-Bajir grunted, like that made perfect sense to him. "My head voice told me to run."

<When? What voice?>

I couldn't see his face, so I couldn't see his expression. Not that I would have known what a Hork-Bajir expression meant, anyway. "Ket Halpak and Jara Hamee at Yeerk pool. Yeerk drained out. Yeerk in pool. Head voice say, '*Run*. Go that way!'"

I sighed and narrowly avoided getting slapped

in the face by a branch. Talking to Hork-Bajir is frustrating.

<You're saying the idea just popped into your head to run away from the Yeerk pool?> I asked.

"Head say, 'Run, Jara Hamee. Take Ket Halpak. Run and be free. Run from Yeerks.' I ask how? How will Jara Hamee and Ket Halpak be free? Head say, 'I will send a guide.'"

<*What?*>

"Head say, 'Run, Jara Hamee —'"

<No, that last part. About a guide.>

"Head voice say, 'I will send a guide.'"

<Who? Me?>

The Hork-Bajir didn't answer. I was quickly coming to realize that Hork-Bajir don't really *get* a lot of things. Speech seems unnatural to them. And it's true, they are not the geniuses of the universe. Which was fine.

But I was getting more and more annoyed by the whole thing. I had been moved around, put in one place or another. Things I couldn't possibly know had popped into my head. I was being used. And I really didn't like the idea of that.

I deeply didn't like the idea of that.

<Okay, that does it. Stop,> I told the two Hork-Bajir.

They stopped. The two big monsters just stood there in the dark between trees and waited.

"We go now?"

<No.>

"Taxxons coming."

<Yep,> I said. <I know.>

"We go now?"

<Nope. Not until I get some answers,> I said defiantly. <This little parade stops right here until I get some —>

By the time I'd said <answers> I was not in the forest anymore. I was not anywhere. Not anywhere I could understand, at least.

I felt myself floating. Hanging in the air, only there wasn't any air. I wasn't flying, just floating.

There was light, a beautiful blue-green sort of light. It didn't come from any one place, though. It just seemed to be coming from everywhere at once.

One thing was for sure — I was not in the forest anymore.

HELLO, TOBIAS. WE MEET AGAIN.

The voice was huge, but not harsh. It filled my brain and seemed to resonate throughout my body. My feathers quivered. My fingers tingled.

Fingers?

And only then did I begin to realize that I was changed.

I looked down at my body. And somehow, in a way I can't explain, I seemed to be seeing *through* my body, too. It was as if I could see everything, from every angle at once. Like I was seeing myself through a million different eyes.

I was no longer a red-tailed hawk. But I was not human, either. At least not the way I had once been human.

I had arms that were wings. I had legs that ended in talons. I had a beak, but it was a mouth, too.

I know this all sounds crazy. I know it's impossible to really imagine it very well. But somehow I was both a human and a bird and some third thing that was in between the two.

We had seen many incredible things since we'd first found a dying Andalite prince in an abandoned construction site. I've seen Yeerks and all their tools — the Taxxons, the Gedds, the Hork-Bajir. I've seen Andalites and met the Chee, the androids in human form. I've traveled through time and to the Yeerk pool and into orbit in spaceships.

But there was only one species that could do this. Only one species that could own that huge head-filling voice.

"The Ellimist," I said in an actual voice that came from my own mouth.

Then, from the vague turquoise fog around me, I saw it flying toward me. It was a bird of prey. A raptor. Some undefinable shape, part falcon, part eagle, part hawk. It had a snow-white belly and reddish-brown back and a tail that spread to show a dusky rainbow of colors.

The bird flew to me, then stopped and floated in midair.

YES, TOBIAS. ELLIMIST. OR AT LEAST *AN* ELLIMIST.

It laughed and the whole turquoise universe laughed along.

"So *you're* the puppet master," I said. "I should have known. But this isn't how you looked last time we saw you."

The bird shape smiled. Don't ask me how it smiled with a beak. It just did. I CHOSE A SHAPE YOU WOULD IDENTIFY WITH.

"Baloney. You know better than that. You know I'm human."

ARE YOU? YOU DON'T LOOK LIKE A HUMAN TO ME.

I felt a queasiness in my stomach. I looked at the body I had. A body that was equal parts boy and bird.

"What do you want from me? Why are you making me do things I don't want to do?"

WHAT HAVE I MADE YOU DO, TOBIAS?

"You put me in places I don't want to be. You've dragged me into this stupid mess with these two Hork-Bajir."

The Ellimist dissolved from bird to human. But not entirely human. He was a human with wings. He looked like I did at that moment. And when he spoke again, it was with a simple, human voice.

"Once I put you and your friends in a position to give your own former species a chance. I looked deep into the future, and found a way to help you — without using my power directly. And now, you are in a position to help the Hork-Bajir. Do they not deserve the same chance as humans?"

"You're trying to save the Hork-Bajir race from the Yeerks?"

The Ellimist smiled again and shook his head. "We do not interfere. We do not use our power for one species against another."

"Bull," I said.

The Ellimist let that go with just a faint smile. "I will not force you, Tobias. And I will not guarantee you will even succeed. There is every chance you will die and the two Hork-Bajir will die, and all will have been a waste."

"Thanks. That really cheers me up," I said. "Why me? Why stick me with this job? What am I, some kind of hero?"

The Ellimist didn't laugh. "Tobias, you are a beginning. You are a point on which an entire time line may turn."

I guess that should have made me feel important. But it didn't. I wasn't interested in being flattered.

"You want my help?" I asked the Ellimist. "Fine. Then I want yours. You're just about all-powerful, according to Ax. You can make entire galaxies disappear if you want. I don't know why you don't just make things happen the way you want them to. But, hey, whatever." I looked him right in the eyes. Right into eyes that were a disturbing mirror image of my own.

"You want me to lead these Hork-Bajir to this place you've put in my head? Fine. But I want to get paid for my services."

"And what do you want, Tobias?"

"You *know* what I want," I said, almost choking on the words. "You *know.*"

"Yes. But do *you* know what you want, Tobias?" the Ellimist asked. "And if you get it, will you still know?"

And suddenly, without any sensation of movement, I was back in the dark of the forest.

CHAPTER 16

It was a long night. I can tell you that for sure. A very long night. Even the Hork-Bajir were worn out by the time the first faint gray of predawn started to appear.

The whole time I was waiting to see a bunch of Taxxons suddenly show up, followed by heavily armed Hork-Bajir. Or else Visser Three in one of his awful morphs. Every shadow looked like it could be an enemy.

And I had other enemies in the forest to worry about. I was extremely aware of the fact that any number of other birds and various hungry mammals were noticing me and thinking maybe I'd make a nice snack.

But I was riding atop a Hork-Bajir. And none

of the forest predators could quite figure out how to deal with that. At one point a pair of wolves, probably scouting for their pack, stood a few dozen yards away and watched us pass.

Wolves are very smart animals. They didn't know what the Hork-Bajir were. But they knew for sure they didn't want to mess with them.

Deer scampered away from us. Owls dismissed us. We were obviously not mice, and that's all the owls cared about. Foxes slunk away. Raccoons froze. Only the forest's most fearless creature ignored us and went on about its business.

In fact, I had to stop Ket Halpak from stepping on one.

<Stop! Stop! Nobody move!> I yelled, having seen the warning stripes of this most fearsome animal.

"Yeerks?" Jara Hamee responded.

"Taxxons?" Ket Halpak asked fearfully.

<No. Worse. A skunk. Just let it go on its way. Nobody move a muscle till it's gone.>

"Hah! Small animal! Not kill Jara Hamee!"

<No, it won't kill you. It'll just make you wish you were dead.>

I didn't know how much ground we had covered by the time we finally took a rest. I can't judge distances on the ground very well anymore. All I knew was that the sky was a shade lighter than absolute black. And the Hork-Bajir had started to stumble a lot. They were beat. And I was starving.

<Do you need something to eat?> I asked the two Hork-Bajir.

"We eat," Jara Hamee agreed. Without any delay, he walked over to a tree. A pine of some sort. He drew back and slashed at the tree trunk with his elbow blade.

SCCCRRAAACK!

He sliced it straight up, opening about a three-foot gash in the bark. With his wrist blade, he began to slice the bark away in chunks ranging from a few inches long to almost a foot square.

He tossed slabs of the stripped bark to his mate and took some for himself.

<That's what you eat?>

"Yes."

<Is that how you eat back on your own world?>

He chewed the bark and seemed to be looking far off. "When Jara Hamee small, Jara Hamee eat from the *Kanver*. Eat from the *Lewhak*. Eat from the tall *Fit Fit*."

<Are those all trees? I mean, are they like these trees?>

"Better," Ket Halpak said.

"Better," Jara Hamee agreed.

I got the feeling Jara thought he might have

insulted me by dissing Earth trees. "Earth tree good," he added.

"Earth tree good," Ket Halpak agreed.

It made me smile inside. There were times when my life was just so utterly insane I could only laugh. A pair of goblins from some far-distant planet were worried they'd hurt my feelings because they didn't like pine bark.

Then, like a light going off in my head, I realized something. <Jara, Ket? Is that why Hork-Bajir have blades? To strip the bark from trees?>

Ket Halpak stood up. I was sitting on a rotting log, so she towered above me like a skyscraper. She pointed to her elbow blade. "For straight cut." Indicating her wrist blade, she said, "For taking off."

Sticking out her knee, she explained, "For down by ground."

<For the bottom of trees,> I said. <Each of the blades has a special use. Each one is for harvesting tree bark.>

"Yes."

She sat back down and took another chunk of bark.

<They aren't weapons? You don't use them to defend yourselves from enemies? To kill prey?>

Jara Hamee looked right at me. "Hork-Bajir have no enemy. No prey. Hork-Bajir not kill.

Yeerk kill. Yeerk kill Andalite. Andalite kill Yeerk. Hork-Bajir die."

<You're caught in the middle. But that's why the Yeerks took over your race — the blades. They made you deadly, once the Yeerk evil was in your head. You're the ultimate soldiers. All because you're adapted to eating tree bark.>

The Hork-Bajir had nothing else to say. They went back to eating.

<Look, I have to go for a while. I . . . um, I have to go get food, too.>

Ket Halpak held out a chunk of bark. "Our food yours."

<Thanks. But I need a different food.>

I didn't tell them what I ate or how I got it.

You know, it's strange. I never feel guilty about being a predator when I'm with humans. After all, good old Homo sapiens is the king of all predators.

But these deadly looking Hork-Bajir were not predators at all. Despite their looks, they were no more dangerous than a deer with a large rack of antlers.

They were just victims. Just a species that had the bad luck to look fearsome. And now they were caught up in a war between Yeerks and the rest of the free species of the galaxy.

I thought of all the battles we'd had with

Hork-Bajir. They had come close to killing me more than once. I had hated and feared them. Now I just felt sorry for them.

And I felt sorrier still, because I knew that my friends and I would fight against Hork-Bajir again in the future.

<I'll be back in half an hour or so,> I said as I took wing. <Don't worry. I won't leave you.>

CHAPTER 17

As I flew up through the trees, I saw the sun just peeking up over the rim of the earth in the east. It instantly lit the treetops with gold. It was a beautiful sight. Golden leaves and dark shadows beneath, and clouds all red on one side and still night-gray on the other.

It felt good to be up off the ground. It felt good to have air beneath my wings and a cold clean breeze in my face. I'd spent the night clinging to a Hork-Bajir's horns and slogging through the brush. That was no place for a bird. Or even for a human in bird shape.

The air was still flat, no thermals, no updrafts, so I had to work hard. But it felt good, flapping my wings and stretching my cramped muscles.

I would miss this when I became human again. Would the Ellimist give me back my human body and let me keep the morphing power? I hoped so. I'd hate to think I would never fly again.

Below me I spotted an opening. Not even a meadow, really, just a small clearing with tall grass and fallen logs and the telltale burrow openings of rats and voles and other tasty morsels.

But I had to be careful. This clearing probably belonged to someone. Another hawk, possibly. Not to mention other species.

I had to get in and out fast. Get in, make my kill, and bail.

I swept the ground with my laser-sharp eyes, looking for the tiny movements that would betray a mouse or a rat. Sometimes, when the light is just right and the hunger is sharp, it's almost like I can see right through the ground. Like I can see the mice in their warm burrows.

Maybe that's why I didn't see the danger. Maybe it was because I was totally focused on eating.

I did spot a rat, though. A nice, plump thing, waddling along toward his own breakfast. I dived from up high.

Then I hit a sudden air pocket! It threw me off-balance and I nearly splattered myself into the dirt. I yanked back just in time and lost my rat.

<Oh, man!> I complained. <Whatever happened to the good old days, when breakfast was a nice easy bowl of Wheaties?>

Well, it would be that way again soon. As soon as the Ellimist kept his promise to me. A warm bed at night and a nice, easy breakfast in the morning.

Not that that's how it had been when I was human. I hadn't exactly been in a nice, normal family. See, both my folks left a long time ago. After that I just got passed around from one aunt or uncle to another.

When I was stuck in morph and disappeared from the human world, I don't even know if any of them looked for me.

I shoved those thoughts aside. I flapped my wings, ready for takeoff. But I just cleared the tops of the tall grasses when —

WHAM!

I was hit! It was like someone had thrown a brick at me. I was down, fluttering in the grass, beating my wings in terror.

What hit me? What the . . . what the heck was happening?

And only then did I see it poking through the

99

grass — an intelligent, curious face, tawny fur, four big paws, and a body that might have been three feet long from its nose to the end of the weirdly curved, short tail that gave the beast its name.

Bobcat!

The wind had been knocked out of me, and I practically fell apart when I saw the big cat.

It circled around me, watching me curiously. Wondering if I would fight back. Calm brown and gold eyes surveyed me as I would survey a wounded rat.

The hawk in me wanted to flap its wings and try to scare the cat away. But the human in me knew I'd have only one chance. I was fast, but the bobcat was like lightning. And it was powerful. It had hit me with one big paw and knocked me silly. A blow that was so graceful it had almost seemed to be slow motion. And yet it was so fast I hadn't had a chance to even *think* about dodging.

How had I been so careless? How could I have missed a bobcat in the bushes? Now I was going to die because of my carelessness.

I stood on my talons, awkward and helpless on the ground. But as I stood my ground, I closed one talon around a stick. It was a bare twig really, no more than two feet long.

I stared hard at the bobcat. It could already

taste hawk meat. If I moved, it would lunge. If I didn't move, it would still lunge.

One chance . . . one small, desperate chance. I had to hit its eyes before it could sink its teeth into me.

The hawk in my head screamed *Fly! Fly! Fly!*

But the human in me said no. The hawk couldn't win this fight. Only the human could. I clutched the stick tightly.

Lunge! The bobcat flew at me.

I jerked back, bringing the stick up off the ground.

"Yowwwrrr!" the bobcat howled as the sharp stick poked his left eye.

<Okay, *now* we can fly!> I flapped and I motored my little taloned feet along the ground and I hauled like I've never hauled before.

But the cat was after me. One step. Two steps, and it had caught up with me! Then it stopped. It turned. I saw it stare. I saw its back fur rise in alarm.

Over the bobcat loomed a shape as big around as a redwood tree. Three rows of tiny, weak claws snapped and clawed at the air. The gigantic centipede head drew back, and I could see two of the red-jelly eye clusters.

Taxxon!

Down came the round red mouth!

Down on the bobcat! And the Taxxon swallowed the cat in a single bite before the shocked animal could figure out what to do.

I was already flapping my way clear of the ground. Thorns and twigs and raspy grass ripped at me, pulling out feathers, but I didn't care about a few feathers right then.

I found a breeze and I thanked Mother Nature for giving me wings. I shot up and up and up till I was at treetop level. Only then did I even look back.

They were crawling across the clearing and through the trees. A dozen of them. Taxxons! Out in daylight. Out where some unlucky hiker could see them.

It was insane! Totally insane!

Behind the Taxxon trackers marched a virtual army of Hork-Bajir warriors. And with the Hork-Bajir were dozens of human-Controllers, all armed to the teeth.

It hit me then with full force. The Yeerks didn't care about being careful. The Yeerks were going to capture the two fugitive Hork-Bajir. No matter the cost. No matter who died.

It was pure Yeerk ruthlessness unleashed.

This was an army. An entire army against me and two decent, simple, and not-very-bright Hork-Bajir.

And I still hadn't had breakfast.

CHAPTER 18

I was shaking pretty badly by the time I got back up into the blue. And then the first thing I saw was a peregrine falcon riding high.

Peregrines won't usually mess with hawks, but I wasn't exactly feeling cocky right at that moment. I didn't need any more trouble. I just wanted to get back to my two Hork-Bajir and get us all out of there.

<Tobias? Is that you down there, by any chance?>

I breathed a huge sigh of relief. It was Jake.

<Oh, man, am I glad to hear your voice, Jake,> I said. <The woods are full of Taxxons and Hork-Bajir and human-Controllers and anything else the Yeerks can throw at us.>

Not to mention hungry bobcats, I added silently.

<Yeah, we noticed,> Jake said. <They almost marched right into a couple of guys out fishing in one of the streams. We managed to scare the fishermen off, or they'd be Taxxon meat now.>

<*We*? The others are with you?> I searched the sky. Yes. A bald eagle. An osprey. <I see Rachel and either Cassie or Marco,> I said.

<Ax is on the ground. Marco is around somewhere. Oh, there! Above you!>

I looked up just in time to see an osprey come ripping down through a wisp of low clouds in a stoop.

<Yee-hah! Tobias!> Marco yelled giddily. <Gotcha!>

<This is so *not* the time to be messing with me!> I yelled. <I was about one feather away from being kitty food. And I'm hungry and I'm tired and I'm mad.>

<Chill, Tobias,> Jake said kindly. <You can relax. We're all here to help you now.>

I heard Cassie's thought-speak voice coming from fairly far away. <Tobias, we've been thinking. You know how you seem to keep ending up in just the right place at just the right time?>

<Or just the *wrong* place, depending on how you look at it,> I muttered.

<We're thinking maybe there is some

other . . . power. Some force. Some person inter-fering with you. Kind of manipulating you.>

If it had been anyone but Cassie, I would have probably said something sarcastic. Like <No, duh.> But it's impossible to be sarcastic to Cassie. <Yeah, it definitely is someone messing with me,> I said. <An old friend of ours.>

<Who?>

<It seems the Ellimist is trying to save the Hork-Bajir. Not that he'll admit that.>

<Hmm. Ax was right,> Cassie said. <He guessed it was the Ellimist.>

Rachel was close enough now to communi-cate. <Yeah, and you know how Ax feels about that guy. Or creature. Or whatever the Ellimist is. Ax says to watch your butt. The Ellimist plays games with people.>

I thought of the Ellimist's promise to me. To give me what I most wanted. But when I recalled the conversation, I couldn't exactly remember an actual promise.

I felt a chill in my bones. Had the Ellimist re-ally promised to make me human again?

<Are you okay, Tobias?> Rachel asked. I could tell from her tone that it was a private mes-sage. Only I could hear it.

<Yeah. I guess so,> I said. <The Ellimist says he'll . . . he'll . . . you know. Make me human again.>

Somehow putting it in actual words didn't sound right. And yet that was what I wanted. To be human again. To live like the others. To eat cold cereal and fried eggs for breakfast instead of hunting and killing. To walk. To spend my nights inside, in a bed. To sit down and watch TV. Or just to sit at all.

<Tobias, that would be *so* great!> Rachel said.

<Yeah. But like Ax said, the Ellimist plays games. And we still have to save the Hork-Bajir without getting wiped out ourselves.>

In a thought-speak voice Jake and Cassie and Marco could hear, too, I said, <Follow me, guys. I'll take you to our two alien friends.>

I turned at an angle to the breeze. It was coming up just behind my right wing. It can be hard flying that way if the wind is too strong. You have to keep correcting your direction because the wind will kind of sneak up and push you off-course.

We flew hard and soon left the Yeerk army behind. I spotted the two Hork-Bajir through the trees. They looked like they were talking. Looking closer, I realized they were holding hands.

I felt embarrassed, just dropping out of the sky on them. <Hey, you two,> I said. <I'm coming in. Some friends are with me.>

We landed in the trees. And now we were facing a serious decision. A life-and-death decision. The others were all close to the two-hour time limit. They needed to demorph.

But so far we had not revealed our true species to the Hork-Bajir. If they were ever recaptured by the Yeerks, the Yeerks would have access to everything in their heads. Every memory.

<Jake?> I asked. <What are you guys going to do?>

<It's a big gamble, letting these two know what we are,> he answered.

<I don't mean to get all CIA about this,> Marco said. <But if they know we're human, they can't ever be captured by the Yeerks. I mean —>

<I know what you mean,> I interrupted.

<Probably better to be dead than a Controller, anyway,> Marco said.

<Easy for you to say,> Rachel said.

<Let me talk to them. Jara and Ket are my friends,> I said.

<Hork-Bajir?> Marco crowed. <These two walking Cuisinarts, these two seven-foot-tall lawn mowers, these living razor blades are your *friends*?>

I ignored Marco. I looked at Jara Hamee. <Jara Hamee. I need to know something. If the Yeerks capture you —>

He didn't even let me finish. He flung out a bladed arm, slashing the air. Then, more care-

107

fully, he pointed at his own head. Right at the scar from the cut he'd made. "No more Yeerk here. Free! Or no Jara Hamee. No Ket Halpak. Only free!"

"Free or dead," Ket Halpak said harshly.

<I see why you like them, Tobias,> Rachel said. She fluttered down from the tree. She began to demorph.

I heard Jake sigh. <Well, I guess we take a chance.>

Within a few minutes everyone was human again. Except me, of course.

I guess we surprised the Hork-Bajir. I don't know what they expected us to be, but it wasn't human. The two big aliens just stood and stared. And then, when they realized what Jake and Rachel and Cassie and Marco actually were, they laughed.

"KeeeRAW! KeeeRAW!"

At least, I think it was laughter. Who knows how a Hork-Bajir laughs?

"Human folk!" Ket Halpak said, sounding amazed and possibly gleeful.

Jara Hamee looked at me. "You human folk?"

<I used to be,> I said. <I, um, well . . . well, I'm not exactly the same as I used to be. I've changed.>

"Jara Hamee change, too. Not free. Now free."

That's when Ax came barreling through the woods and leaped right into the middle of our little group. He was carrying a bag. In the bag were shoes for the others. See, when you morph you can morph tight clothing, but shoes just can't be done.

Ax set the bag down and stared in the way that only an Andalite can stare — in all directions at once.

<This is very dangerous, letting them see what you are,> Ax said heatedly. <These Hork-Bajir can never be recaptured. They can *never* be taken alive now!>

<They won't be,> I said. <They're going to be free.>

"Free or dead!" Jara Hamee yelled.

"Okay, I definitely like these guys," Rachel said. She kind of cocked her head and looked up at Jara Hamee. "Free or dead!" she yelled, just as loudly as the Hork-Bajir had.

Cassie and Jake and I yelled it, too. With slightly less enthusiasm. In my case, I'd been too close to being dead just a few minutes earlier.

"I'll give you two-to-one odds on 'dead,'" Marco said grimly. "And if we all keep yelling with a bunch of Taxxons half a mile away, I'll make it ten-to-one."

Rachel ran over, grabbed Marco by the shoulders and gave him a good hard shake. "Come on, you big baby, say it — free or dead!"

"Yeah, yeah, free or dead," Marco said. Then he laughed. "Rachel, you do know you're insane, right?"

"Yes, but she's a Packard Foundation Outstanding Student who's insane," Cassie chimed in.

"I'm sure the Yeerks will be impressed," Marco said.

Jake smiled a curious smile at me. "Well? Let's get going."

CHAPTER 19

"So where exactly *are* we going?" Marco asked.

<We're going to wherever this valley is. The valley the Ellimist showed me,> I said.

"Should we be singing that valderee, valdera, valderee, valdera-hah-hah-hah-hah-hah song?" Marco asked. "I mean, we are 'a-wandering.'"

"Marco, you should never be singing anything," Rachel said. "I've heard you sing."

We were a strange little parade. After an hour we had reached the lower foothills of the mountains. And for the last two hours we'd been climbing up those hills. Up and up.

Jake, Rachel, Cassie, and Marco were all in

111

their own human bodies. They were walking single file with the two Hork-Bajir behind.

Ax was way out in front, scouting ahead. He was far faster than any of the humans, and faster even than the Hork-Bajir. And Ax would be able to handle it if he happened to bump into some enemy Hork-Bajir.

I flew cover. I did a slow circle that carried me all the way out to where Ax was, then all around the area. That part was hard because there was a steady headwind rolling down from the mountains. On the back side of the circle I would drift around till I could see the first edge of the pursuing Taxxons.

Between Ax and me, we figured we wouldn't be surprised by anything leaping out at us.

But the more we climbed, the higher up the foothill paths we went, the more worried I became. What was the point of leading Jara Hamee and Ket Halpak to some secluded valley if we brought a whole Yeerk army with us?

Did the Ellimist have some clever plan? Probably not. The Ellimist seemed to think he had to do the absolute minimum. He didn't mind sticking his little finger into the time stream, but he didn't exactly jump in all the way. I had the feeling we were on our own.

I drifted above my friends in time to hear Marco complain.

"I'm just saying, hey, is there some reason the Ellimist can't just transport us wherever we're going? This hill-climbing is killing my legs. Up and up and up."

"Are you going to whine the whole way?" Rachel asked.

"Yes," Marco confirmed. "That's the plan. Whine the whole way."

"I think it's nice," Cassie said. "I mean, we're out in nature. Breathing fresh air. No noise or distractions. No TV or stereo blaring. No cars. Just nature. Trees and animals."

"Yeah, I guess you're right, Cassie," Marco said. "What could be more relaxing than going on a hike with a couple of fugitive space goblins while being hunted by giant worms and probably Visser Three himself? And all the time knowing we're following the plan of an all-powerful galactic pain-in-the-butt who gets us to do all his dirty work?"

Cassie grinned. "Yeah, but while we're running from giant worms we're breathing nice, fresh mountain air. Come on, Marco, you could use the exercise." She got behind Marco and started to push him up the hill. "Just keep telling yourself — we're having fun with nature, we're having fun with nature."

"How about this — I'm hungry," Marco said just as I glided out of hearing range.

He was hungry, I was hungry. Everyone was hungry, even the Hork-Bajir, because we couldn't let them strip bark. That would have made it even easier for the Yeerks to follow us.

Then I saw breakfast. Even though it was more like lunchtime. A mouse, sitting right out in the open. It was digging seeds out of a fallen pinecone.

I hesitated only for a moment. Then down I went.

It was a perfect strike.

I felt great. The hawk part of my mind has a pretty simple outlook on life — when it eats, it's happy. And there is a very satisfying sensation that comes from doing a job well. Even when the job is hunting mice.

I was just back above the trees when I saw the disaster looming. And heard that characteristic sound.

FWOMP-FWOMP-FWOMP-FWOMP-FWOMP-FWOMP-FWOMP-FWOMP —

<Helicopters!> I yelled. But the others were all too far away to hear me. I cursed myself. Idiot! Idiot! While you were hunting, the Yeerks brought in helicopters!

There were three of them, spread out over a mile or so. And they were coming up fast.

I flew. But the wind coming down off the mountains was against me, and I could barely make progress. If those choppers flew over my friends, they'd spot them in an instant. They'd see four humans, two big Hork-Bajir and an Andalite. And then everything would be over.

FWOMP-FWOMP-FWOMP-FWOMP-FWOMP-FWOMP-FWOMP —

The helicopters were getting near.

I used every flying trick I knew to get speed. I raced forward every time the breeze slackened. I dropped down below the trees to avoid the stronger gusts. And slowly I advanced.

<Jake! Rachel! If you can hear me, get off the trail and morph!>

They couldn't answer, of course, because they weren't in morph. I had no way of knowing if they'd heard me.

<Jake! Rachel! Cassie! Marco! Helicopters coming!>

And just then, the first helicopter swept over me, roaring and ripping up the air. It was like being caught in a tornado. The rotor wash grabbed me and threw me sideways through the air.

FWOMP-FWOMP-FWOMP-FWOMP-FWOMP-FWOMP-FWOMP —

I hit a branch.

SNAP!

I felt a jolt of pain.

I flapped my wings, but only my right wing worked.

Then it hit me. The snap I'd heard had been my own bone.

I fell through the branches. WHAP! WHAP! WHAP!

I hit the ground and lay there, fluttering weakly, helpless. Helpless, as only a flightless bird can be helpless.

Panic caught me up and carried me along. No! No! My friends needed me. No! I couldn't just lie there on the leaves. No!

And then I saw the end coming for me. Not a bobcat. Not a Taxxon or a Hork-Bajir or a Yeerk of any kind.

Just a humble, ordinary, everyday raccoon.

CHAPTER 20

The raccoon watched me from masked black eyes. I flared my one good wing and snapped with my beak. But the raccoon was too smart and too experienced to fall for my tricks.

It knew I was helpless.

FWOMP-FWOMP-FWOMP-FWOMP-FWOMP —

A second helicopter passed overhead, indifferent to the plight of a crippled hawk.

The raccoon grabbed me by my broken wing and began to drag me. I was on my back, being dragged by an animal not much bigger than a large tabby cat. I snapped again and again, but I couldn't reach the raccoon with my beak. I couldn't turn well enough to bring my talons to bear. And the raccoon knew it.

I heard the gurgling sound of water rushing over stones. Horror filled me. The fear was so terrible I almost fainted. You see, I knew what was coming next.

People say raccoons wash their food. Actually, that's not true. Raccoons do sometimes run water over their food, but it is not about cleanliness.

Raccoons are careful eaters. With their sensitive paws they dig through the meat, feeling for anything they don't want. The water rushing over their paws helps them feel.

The raccoon was going to eat me. And it didn't really care if I was still alive.

<No! No! No!> I screamed to a deaf forest.

I felt ice-cold water flow through my feathers. And I felt the busy fingers of the raccoon.

<No! NOOOOO!>

YOU ASKED ME FOR PAYMENT IN EXCHANGE FOR USING YOU. WOULD YOU LIKE YOUR REWARD NOW?

The Ellimist!

<Now! Now! Yes, now would be a really good time!> I screamed.

IT IS DONE.

<What's done? Nothing is done, you lunatic! I'm still a bird!>

OF COURSE.

<Help me!>

The raccoon was literally looking down at me

like you might look at a steak. He was deciding where to bite first.

THE ANDALITE GAVE YOU POWER. USE IT.

I was too insane with terror to figure out what he was saying at first. Then it dawned on me. <What? What? That's my reward? That's all? You're giving me back my morphing power?>

IT'S WHAT YOU WANTED.

<I wanted to be human again!> I screamed. <You liar! You cheat! I want to be human!>

But the Ellimist said nothing more. And my problem right then was the raccoon. His tiny, razor-sharp teeth were descending toward me. So with my last ounce of self-control, ignoring the searing pain in my wing, I turned just enough to grab one of his hind legs in my weakened talon.

Focus, Tobias, I told myself. *Focus or get eaten.*

I focused. I concentrated with all my will. And to my utter amazement, I saw the raccoon's eyes cloud over. I felt his grip weaken.

And like a miracle, I felt myself begin to "acquire" the raccoon. I felt it become a part of me.

I had morphed only two animals. A cat. And a red-tailed hawk. I had never escaped the red-tailed morph. I didn't have much experience morphing. Not like the others.

And as I concentrated on the raccoon DNA inside me, I felt my beak begin to soften . . . my talons begin to fatten . . . and my wings . . . my glorious wings began to shrink.

The raccoon — I mean the *real* raccoon — recoiled in surprise. He stepped back and stared as I morphed into him.

It wasn't much of a change of size. Raccoons aren't much larger than hawks. But everything else was different. My eyes were growing dim. And suddenly I could smell as well as I could hear.

Feathers were melting into gray and black fur. I was morphing.

I was morphing!

The real raccoon had had enough. He was a smart, wily old scrapper, and he knew better than to hang around in a place where birds turn into raccoons. He waddled away.

I was safe. For now. Safe and becoming something I had never been before. The sharp edge of terror started to recede and I could almost enjoy what was happening.

I was morphing! I had the power again. I wouldn't have to sit on the bench when the others went into danger.

I was back!

But not human.

It's what you wanted. That's what the Ellimist said. But he was a liar. He was a cheat. He had tricked me. I wanted to be human. I wanted to be human again, with my own hands and feet and eyes and mouth.

No time for that now, I told myself. *Get to the others. Hurry!*

I took off at a run. Amazing! It was amazing to be running. To be down at ground level with things rushing past.

The ground was so close below me. It was scary, in a way. I kept thinking, pull up, pull up! In my guts I felt this need for altitude. It's dangerous, flying too close to the ground.

And no matter how I tried to hurry, the raccoon body was not built for speed. It lumbered along. It seemed to need to stop constantly to sniff at this or that.

It wasn't that I couldn't control the body. I could. That part had been fairly easy. I mean, the instincts of the raccoon, the urgent need for food, the fear of predators, all that was normal to me.

I just couldn't get the stubby legs to move fast enough. My friends were half a mile away! I'd never reach them in time to help.

I stopped. I was panting heavily. The raccoon heart was racing. What could I do? What could I do? I'd ended up in a useless morph!

I craned my raccoon head upward. I couldn't see very well, but I knew the sky was up there. I could see a faded sort of blue through the trees.

121

Wait . . . was it possible? Could I remorph back into my own body? My red-tailed body? DNA isn't affected by injuries. If I morphed back to red-tail, I wouldn't have the broken wing.

Would I?

The others had done it. They had morphed out of injured bodies. Then when they re-morphed, the bodies were whole again.

I had to try. It was so stupid! I'd been left out of so many missions because I *couldn't* morph. Now I *could* morph and I was totally useless.

I focused. I closed my weak raccoon eyes and focused on a different body. A body with feathers and wings. And slowly I became myself again.

CHAPTER 21

I flew.

I'd only been without my wings for a few minutes, but still I felt weirded out. I mean, I know the others are used to being in different bodies. But I'm not.

I peered ahead with my hawk sight. I saw no helicopters. I did see a few shaking treetops. Large beasts were moving beneath those trees. Taxxons and Hork-Bajir.

I flew on and soon saw the tail end of the Yeerk search army. Human-Controllers, their human bodies wearing out, staggered up the hill.

Ahead of them, Hork-Bajir warriors. They were stronger and faster than the humans. Their sergeants had to keep holding them back so they wouldn't leave the human-Controllers behind.

And out in front of them all, the Taxxon trackers continued their search.

I flew hard and fast. And then, at last, I saw the helicopters. They were low to the ground. They were spread out in a line abreast. And unless I was totally mistaken, they were past where my friends would be.

I felt a chill of fear. I knew what they were going to do. This time it wasn't the Ellimist telling me what would happen. It was my own predator's instincts. I knew my friends were being hunted. And I knew how the Yeerks would do it.

The helicopters were a mile away, maybe a little more. So I heard nothing of them. But as I watched, I saw the sudden red spear that shot down to the ground.

Again and again and again the helicopters fired their blazing Dracon beams down at dry trees and even dryer underbrush.

They were starting a forest fire!

Within minutes, a wall of smoke was advancing through the trees. The wall of smoke had to be a mile long, end to end. It would block Jake and Rachel and the others. It would stop them and turn them back. Back toward the waiting Taxxons and Hork-Bajir warriors.

As I watched, a flutter of pale brown. Some bird escaping the flames.

A stab of red! The bird flamed and burned in midair!

Had it been one of my friends in morph?

<What am I supposed to do?!> I yelled at the Ellimist. <This is impossible! I can't stop those helicopters. Are you just going to stand by now and do nothing?>

There was no answer. I was not surprised. As Ax had said, the Ellimist was playing his own games. He didn't care if I thought it was fair.

I dropped down, down below treetop level to avoid getting Draconed myself. The wind wasn't as strong down in the trees, but I had the worse problem of having to dodge branches.

And then, just a glimpse below me! A pale blue deer with a scorpion's tail.

<Ax! Ax, it's me, Tobias!>

<Hello, Tobias,> Ax said as calmly as if nothing were happening.

<Where is everyone?>

<They are nearby. We seem to be in a trap.>

<No kidding,> I said. Then, aiming my thought-speak at all my friends, I said, <Everyone keep your heads down. Don't try and fly or anything. The Yeerks are shooting anything that rises above the trees.>

125

I came to rest on a rotting log. I was so exhausted I almost missed my landing and crashed.

A huge brown bear about the size of a minivan came lumbering up.

<Rachel, I really hope that's you, because I've had all the close calls I can stand for one day.>

<It's me, Tobias. Chill. Take a rest. We figure we have maybe five minutes before this whole thing closes on us.>

The two Hork-Bajir appeared, accompanied by Jake in his tiger morph. Cassie and Marco came running from the direction of the helicopters. Cassie's thick gray fur was singed. I could smell the reek of burned hair.

<More helicopters coming up to join those three!> Marco reported. <Oh, hi, Tobias. There you are. I figured you'd flown off to somewhere safe.>

I decided not to take offense. I was just too tired to care what Marco said.

<Jake, there's no way around that wall of fire,> Cassie said breathlessly.

"No Yeerks!" Jara Hamee said fearfully. "Jara Hamee and Ket Halpak free!"

<We'll have to fight!> Rachel said. <We go straight at those Taxxons, blow past them, catch the Hork-Bajir by surprise, no problem. We can . . .>

126

She stopped. Even she didn't believe what she was saying.

<They won't stop till Jara and Ket are dead,> Jake said flatly. <The Yeerks are not going to give up. They are flat-out never going to allow two Hork-Bajir to escape.>

<I guess it would set a bad example,> Marco said. But he wasn't making a joke. <If two get away, who knows? Maybe others will try. The Yeerks can't allow that. They need the Hork-Bajir to be without hope. They need them to be convinced there's no way out.>

<Marco is right,> Cassie said. <Look at the risks the Yeerks are taking! I mean, geez, they've started a forest fire. They have Taxxons and Hork-Bajir all over this forest. They've gone nuts.>

"Jara Hamee and Ket Halpak free!" Jara Hamee said again. It was as if he was trying to convince himself.

<Wait a minute,> I said. <Wait a minute. What you said, Jake! What you said — they won't give up till Jara and Ket are dead.>

<Yeah? So?> Jake asked. Then I guess he realized what I was thinking. <Hey! Rachel has already morphed Jara. Hey, are you thinking what I'm thinking?>

<Yeah,> I said. <At least I think I am. When I was flying I saw a deep ravine. We should still be

able to reach it! It should be perfect. But we'll need Marco in gorilla morph.>

<We will? You lost me there, dude,> Jake said. <But, okay. If you say so, Tobias. Marco in gorilla morph. What else?>

<And we need someone to acquire and morph Ket,> I said.

<I'll do it,> Jake said without hesitation.

<No, Jake. Not this time,> I said. <I'll do it.>

No one said anything for a good thirty seconds. They just stared. They stared with wolf eyes and bear eyes and tiger eyes and all four Andalite eyes. They were trying to decide if I was crazy.

<You *will?*> Rachel asked. <*You* will?>

<Yeah. I will. I'll morph Ket. I'll morph a Hork-Bajir.>

Then Rachel clicked. <The Ellimist? That's what he did for you? I thought he was going to make you human again.> There was an edge of anger in her tone. Of outrage.

<Ellimists,> Ax practically spit the word. <Never trust them.>

<Oh, no,> Cassie whispered. <That's it? He gave you back the power to morph? But not . . .>

<No,> I said as evenly as I could. <Looks like I'm a full member of the team again. I can morph. But I guess . . . I mean, it looks like I'll still be a hawk. I'll be keeping my wings.>

CHAPTER 22

I quickly told them the details of my plan. I had to stick to business. There was no time for feeling sorry for myself. And I sure didn't want them feeling sorry for me.

No time for pity. No time for anger, either. There was nothing I could do to the Ellimist. Nothing I could do.

<Okay, Cassie? We need you to stay in wolf morph. Ax, watch Cassie's back and try to stay out of view. Marco? You know your part, right?>

"Yeah, I got it," he said nervously. He was temporarily human. In between morphs.

Marco's part of the plan was one of the most difficult. And if he failed, Rachel and I were dead. <No problem, right?> I said to Marco.

"Yeah. No problem. Just make sure one of you is a few seconds behind the other. I'll need some time."

<I know my role,> Jake said. He was just coming out of his tiger morph. <Up in the air.>

<My old job,> I said.

"Yeah. Let's hope I do it as well as you always did," Jake said. "Cassie, Ax. Let's move it. Marco, quit worrying. It's just like catching a pass with your eyes closed. No big deal for Mighty Marco."

Marco laughed. "That's it, flatter me. Now I *know* we're dead. But don't worry, I'll be there."

I fluttered over to stand on Ket Halpak's shoulder. (It isn't easy to find a place to sit on a Hork-Bajir.) I dug my talons in just a bit to the dark, leathery skin. And I began to acquire the Hork-Bajir's DNA.

All around I could hear the sounds of enemies closing in. I heard the FWOMP-FWOMP-FWOMP of the helicopters. And now that they were getting closer, my hawk hearing could even detect the faint TSEEEW! TSEEEW! of the Dracon beams.

Sometimes there would come a loud crack, almost like sudden thunder. It was the sound of a tree exploding as the Dracon beam turned the tree sap to steam in a split second.

And there was the roar of the fire itself.

But I shut all of that out of my mind. All I had to focus on was acquiring the Hork-Bajir. Ket Halpak went slightly limp. I could feel the muscles relaxing.

At last, I flew away to a bare spot on the forest floor. The others were all watching me, even while they did their own morphs. I think they halfway suspected I was nuts. They halfway wondered if I'd just made it up about being able to morph.

I closed my eyes and held the image of the Hork-Bajir in my mind. And then, very quickly, I began to feel the changes.

I sprouted up from the pine needles and dead leaves. I rocketed up and up so fast I couldn't help but yell.

<Yah! Whoa! Whoa!>

<Hey! He *is* morphing,> Marco said.

<I guess that's something, at least,> Rachel said bitterly.

I ignored her angry tone. I couldn't listen to her anger because it would just make me mad, too. A predator is never angry, just hungry. Anger only gets in the way.

Up and up I grew. And as I grew, my wings grew with me. It's funny the way morphing works. It's never totally logical. It's never exactly the same twice, either.

And it is always, always gross. Even as I was

morphing, I was watching the others undergo changes. It was a scene out of some lunatic's darkest nightmare. Bodies melted. Weird appendages grew suddenly, here and there. Teeth appeared before there was a mouth to hold them. Fur grew like one of those time-lapse videos of mold, just shooting out of the skin. Big humans tottered unsteadily on tiny doglike legs.

If you just happened to wander in and saw the spectacle of four kids and a bird all melting and mutating and squirming as two giant aliens watched, you'd definitely think you were insane. You'd want to see a psychiatrist. After you stopped screaming.

I could feel the changes happening in my own body. Not that they were painful. They weren't. But I could still feel things going on. And I could hear them.

My insides were reorganizing totally. Hork-Bajir have at least two hearts, maybe more. So entire new hearts were forming inside of me. And from the hearts, new arteries and veins had to sprout and spread throughout my body.

I had to go from having a digestive system designed to handle big chunks of raw mouse to a digestive system built for tree bark.

I could hear a gurgling sound as internal organs shifted and stretched and were pushed aside to make room for totally new organs. I could hear a stretching, grinding sound as big, thick, solid bones replaced my hollow bird bones.

And on the outside I saw my wings grow till they were huge. Then, with amazing speed, the feathers melted into hard, leathery skin. There was a snap as the joints in my wings changed direction to bend the way a Hork-Bajir arm bends.

Then out came the blades.

SHWOOP! Blades at my wrists.

SHWOOP! Blades at my elbows.

SHWOOP! The forward-swept horn blades on my snake head.

<Hey, Tobias,> Marco said. <You kept the same feet.>

It was a joke. But it was true, too. There wasn't much difference between my hawk talons and the feet of the Hork-Bajir. Except that they were maybe a hundred times bigger.

Somehow that made me feel good. I liked the look of those big, ripping talons. I liked thinking about what they would do to a Taxxon.

Cassie and Ax took off at a run. They had a lot of distance to cover very fast. Fortunately, a wolf can run almost flat-out all day long. And there's no doubt about how fast an Andalite can move. No doubt. Jara Hamee and Ket Halpak left with them.

Marco was in his huge, powerful gorilla morph

and getting ready to leave, too. <See you guys later. I hope,> he said.

<Be there!> Rachel growled. She pointed a dangerous Hork-Bajir hand at him.

<Okay, I'll be there. But don't be too long or I may decide to take a nap,> Marco joked as he lumbered off through the trees.

Jake was perched on a branch just over my head. A peregrine falcon, the fastest thing in the air. He spread his wings and took off, leaving me and Rachel alone.

Rachel had morphed into a mirror image of me. We were a fine pair of Hork-Bajir.

<Ready?> I asked her.

She peered at me from behind alien eyes. <You okay, Tobias?>

<Sure. Why wouldn't I be?>

<Well, you haven't exactly had a great day,> she said.

I laughed grimly. <I'm a freak of nature, Rachel. Any day I stay alive is a good day for me.>

CHAPTER 23

Ηigh above the treetops Jake flew in his swift peregrine falcon morph, calling down directions to Rachel and me.

It was weird. It almost felt like Jake had taken over my role or something. Like he was pretending to be me. Normally, I'd be the one up there riding the wind.

<Okay, not far now,> Jake said. <You're almost there. You guys know which direction to go after the Yeerks catch your trail, right?>

<Yeah, we know, we know, *Mother*,> Rachel said. <What are we? Idiots?> Then to me she said, <We do know, right?>

<I'm pretty sure. I mean, it's harder to keep track of where things are when you're down on

the ground. Just trees and bushes everywhere. You can't see the horizon, you can't see the sun.>

The forest was impossible for a Hork-Bajir trying to be quiet. I mean, we could have slashed our way through the brambles and thorn thickets, but that would have attracted too much attention too soon.

So we tried to hurry, but without making too much noise. And let me tell you — Hork-Bajir bodies are not built for quiet.

<That's why you have me up here,> Jake said cheerfully. <To guide you. Don't sweat it. I can see the ravine. I can see that Cassie and Ax and the two Hork-Bajir are getting into position. And I see Marco. Heck, with these falcon eyes I can practically see Marco's fleas.>

<Easy for you to be cocky,> I muttered. <You're up there safe.>

<Do you see the line of fire?> Rachel asked Jake. <Because I sure do smell it.>

<Yeah,> Jake admitted. <In fact, the fire forms a semicircle around you. The Taxxons and friends are the other half of the circle. The only way open is the ravine. So we're just going to get one chance.>

<Wonderful,> I said.

<Okay, you guys. A big, fat pair of Taxxons are just on the other side of that pile of rocks.>

<What pile of rocks?> Rachel asked.

<Oh . . . well, I can see that it's a pile of rocks from up here. From where you are it probably just looks like a thick tangle of weeds and thorns.>

<Cool,> Rachel said calmly. <I guess it's time.>

<Yep. Ladies first.>

<No, no. After you. I insist.>

We pushed our way through the bushes and climbed to the top of what did turn out to be a pile of rock boulders. At the top we stopped and stared.

Just twenty feet away were two Taxxons. Two vile, disgusting Taxxons. Allies, not just slaves, of the Yeerks. A species that ate its own when given half a chance.

I don't know if it was the hawk in me that was angered by the sight of the two humongous worms marching through a decent forest, or the human side of me that just didn't like gigantic worms, period, or some deep instinct of the Hork-Bajir mind. But I was suddenly filled with hatred and rage.

The anger hit me like a baseball bat alongside the head. It was sudden and ferocious. The plan was to run from the Taxxons. But all of a sudden, I didn't want to run.

I wanted to see what my Hork-Bajir blades would do. I wanted to hurt the Taxxons.

137

<Let's take 'em,> I said.

Rachel turned her snake head toward me. <What? That's not the plan, Tobias!>

<They shouldn't be here. Look at them! Look at them, slithering through the forest like they own it! They shouldn't be here. This isn't their place, it's ours. It's mine!>

<Tobias, calm down. It makes me mad, too. But we have to stick with the plan.>

<No. We don't,> I said. <I'm tired of plans.>

Rachel grabbed my shoulder. I almost spun around and slashed at her. That's how mad I was. My arm actually came up as if I were going to strike.

But Rachel didn't back away. <Look, Tobias. You're mad. But it's not the time or place. The person you're mad at is beyond your reach. You can't get back at the Ellimist for betraying you.>

Somehow her words penetrated the black rage that had swallowed me up. No, I couldn't get back at the Ellimist. And it was him I was furious with. Wasn't it? Rachel was right. She had to be right.

It was the Ellimist's fault.

<Stick to the plan, Tobias. Don't get us all killed because you're mad at the Ellimist.>

<Yeah. You're right. The plan.>

Rachel released my shoulder. I stared down at the Taxxons. They had frozen on seeing us. They knew they were no match for a couple of desperate Hork-Bajir.

But then, through the woods, shadowy figures appeared. Hork-Bajir warriors. Hork-Bajir-Controllers.

"Ssssrrrreyyyaa ssseewwwitt!" the Taxxons shrilled in their own hissing language.

From the trees a dozen Hork-Bajir suddenly broke at full run.

<Outta here!> Rachel yelled.

<Right behind you!>

We bolted. And we no longer had to worry about being too obvious. The Hork-Bajir were after us, and we had to use maximum speed to escape.

<The plan seems to be working so far,> Jake called down.

<Yeah. They're on us,> Rachel said.

We ran through the bushes like only Hork-Bajir can run. Our arms slashed the air, again and again, quick as striking snakes. We destroyed bushes and saplings like a pair of out-of-control, nuclear-powered lawn mowers.

SLASH! SLASH! SLASH! SLASH!

But there was one big problem with doing what we were doing. See, we were slowed down a little by having to cut our way through. And the Hork-Bajir behind us could just follow our trail.

<They're gaining on you!> Jake said.

139

<Yeah, we noticed. How far to the ravine?>

<Too far! You won't make it this way.>

<Well, *find* a way!> I yelled. I could see the pursuing Hork-Bajir. Their horn blades were bobbing above the undergrowth. They were not far behind us. Not far, as in pretty soon I'd be smelling their bad breath.

<I . . . I can't tell what anything is from up here,> Jake cried. <It's like reading a map or something. What should I be looking for?>

<We need to go at an angle,> I said. <Look for a gully or ditch that runs across our path. The deeper the better.>

<Oh. Nothing! Wait. Maybe that's a gully. There's a little stream running down it.>

<Just tell us left or right!> I yelled.

<Okay. Left! No! No! I was thinking my left. Go right! Okay, ten more steps . . .>

The Hork-Bajir were on us. In seconds they'd have us in clear view.

<There!> Jake yelled.

<Yeah!> I said. We hit a tiny, shallow stream. It was almost hidden by overhanging vines and drooping branches. <This way, Rachel.>

I crouched as low as my massive, stiff Hork-Bajir body could go, and I ran bent over along the stream. Rachel was inches behind me.

<Ow!> she yelped.

<What?>

<Your tail caught me in the neck. Never mind! Run! Run!>

Behind us I could hear the noise of the pursuing Hork-Bajir grow louder, then slowly more distant.

<All right!> Jake said. <You lost them. Now you have to cut left to get back toward the ravine.>

Up and out of the gully we leaped. Back on dry ground we found some nice, open country beneath very tall trees.

<Oh, man, this isn't good,> Jake said.

<What? Tell me.>

<The fire is sweeping right down the lip of the ravine from the north! And the Yeerks are closing the gap from the south!>

<What do we do?> I asked.

<Look, there's no way around this, Tobias. There's a line of Hork-Bajir now between you two and the ravine. You have to go through them.>

<Hope you haven't lost all that anger,> Rachel said to me. <Looks like we fight, after all.>

CHAPTER 24

On our left, fire!

On our right, the front ranks of Taxxons!

Straight ahead, a ravine a hundred feet deep. It was like it had been cut with a knife. Like someone had slashed the earth and made a cut so deep you could throw a skyscraper down it.

The ravine was narrow, no more than forty feet across. At the bottom, I knew, was a rushing stream. In spring it would swell with the melting ice from the mountains.

But now the stream was narrow, leaving wide sandy banks on either side.

<You're only about fifteen, twenty seconds away from the ravine!> Jake called down. <But there are more bad guys getting in the way. I'm

pretty sure I count six. Two Taxxons and four Hork-Bajir warriors.>

<Oh, man,> I muttered.

Fifteen seconds, Jake had said. I counted in my head as I ran. *One . . . two . . . three . . . four . . .*

"HeeeRRRROWWRRR!"

A Hork-Bajir warrior leaped at me, a blur of dark green-black leather skin and flashing blades. Then more of them. They were everywhere!

<Rachel! Behind you!>

SLASH! A wrist blade drew a line of blood across my chest.

SLASH! I fought back, hacking at my attacker with all my speed and strength.

<AHHHH!> The pain came out of nowhere! A Hork-Bajir had jumped up from the deep grass and hit me from behind. I could feel my entire left side starting to go numb.

SLASH!

SLASH!

SLASH! My wrist blades and elbow blades ripped into Hork-Bajir flesh. I went a little crazy, I think, because I didn't even know what I was doing anymore. I was on automatic. I was a slashing, ripping, tearing machine.

But I was getting hurt at the same time. I was outnumbered. There were three Hork-Bajir on me. Two on Rachel. There had been three on her, too, but she'd taken one of them out of the fight.

SLASH! SLASH! SLASH! My entire world was nothing but blow and counterblow. A wrist blade cut toward my head, and I blocked it. I swiped upward with my knee, and then jerked my talons back to catch the thigh of the Hork-Bajir behind me.

Every move happened in a split second. In the time it would take a human to blink his eyes once, I would block two thrusts and throw three of my own.

Then . . . WHAM! I was on my back in the dirt. My left leg had stopped working! Two Hork-Bajir now stood over me. One raised his ripping talon, ready to bring it down on my chest!

I lay back helpless, staring up at the blue sky.

Suddenly, a flash of pale gray, coming down like a rock! Like an arrow fired from a cloud it came, wings tucked back, dropping at more than a hundred miles an hour.

A peregrine falcon. The fastest thing in the air.

Jake!

At the last second, his wings opened, he took the shock of the air and he swept his talons forward, all in one fluid movement.

Even in pain, lying there a second away from

death, I thought I had never seen anything so perfect in my life.

In a split second Jake was gone, and the larger Hork-Bajir was screaming and holding his eyes.

I was ready. I swept my leg left to right and knocked the Hork-Bajir off his feet. I was up and hobbling on my one good leg before he hit the ground.

I ran to Rachel and helped knock her last Hork-Bajir foe to the ground.

<Ready to go?>

<Been ready,> Rachel said.

Although my one leg was almost useless, I could still use my tail for balance and hobble at a pretty good speed. Rachel soon pulled out ahead of me. But that was okay. That was the plan.

<Jake?> I said. <That was one sweet save back there. Would it be wrong for me to say I love you, man?>

<Hah-HAH! That was fun! Oh, yeah. Oh, yeah, that was a rush!> Jake exulted.

Rachel and I ran toward the lip of the ravine. And now I could actually feel the heat of the fire approaching. The wind shifted and I gagged on thick black smoke. I lost sight of Rachel.

When the smoke cleared, I was face-to-face with a Taxxon. <You're lucky I'm in a hurry, or

you'd be worm hash,> I said, and brushed past the huge centipede.

<Rachel! Ten feet to your left,> Jake instructed. <Yeah! Yeah! Right there between the two saplings!>

I looked forward just in time to see Rachel leap out into the air. Out into the emptiness she went . . . and then disappeared. She fell from sight.

My hearts stopped beating. Both of them. I felt my throat clutch tight.

It was a hundred feet to the bottom of that ravine. Not even a Hork-Bajir could survive that kind of fall.

Now it was my turn. I ran for the ravine lip.

<Oh, man!> Jake cried. <On your left! In front of you! I didn't see them all in the smoke! Tobias, it's him!>

A thick wall of smoke swirled around me, then blew away. It was like some horrible magic trick. One minute, there was the ravine. The next second, there stood three Hork-Bajir. And one Andalite.

One Andalite who was no Andalite at all.

Visser Three stood on the very lip of the ravine. Right in my path.

Hork-Bajir are fast. But the tail of an Andalite is faster. I couldn't win a fight against Visser Three and three Hork-Bajir. No way.

But then it suddenly occurred to me . . .

I grinned. At least as much as a Hork-Bajir can grin. I looked Visser Three right in his main eyes.

"Ket Halpak free!" I yelled, using my Hork-Bajir voice.

And I charged straight at him, running flat-out, ignoring the searing pain from my injured leg.

Visser Three watched me calmly for a couple of seconds. Then it occurred to him, too. Just like it had to me. See, he might get me with his tail, and even kill me before I could get to the ravine, but my momentum would certainly carry me forward.

And I would knock Visser Three off the edge, too.

At the last second, Visser Three dodged nimbly out of my way.

"Ket Halpak and Jara Hamee freeeeeeee!" I shouted defiantly as I jumped off the edge of the ravine.

I fell.

The floor of the ravine was a long, long, *long* way down.

I saw a brutish, massive arm shoot out. A fist the size of a Virginia baked ham grabbed my leg.

I stopped falling. I slammed into the ravine wall. And the massive arm yanked me back upward. Right up into the shallow cave in the ravine wall.

No Earth animal could possibly have caught a falling, seven-foot-tall Hork-Bajir in midair. No animal except a gorilla.

<Nice catch,> I said to Marco.

He hauled me up into the cave and bodily shoved me back to where Rachel was waiting quietly.

We huddled there. Waiting. Silent. We were just a few feet down below the lip of the ravine.

Because of the overhang, I could look down and see the floor of the ravine. Down there, on the sand, lay the crumpled forms of two very dead-looking Hork-Bajir. A pair of hungry wolves were already tearing at their "dead" flesh.

Jara Hamee and Ket Halpak lay still as Cassie and Jake, who had to fly down to the ravine and morph from falcon to human to wolf, pretended to begin devouring them. Fortunately, Hork-Bajir can stand a lot of pain. And they heal quickly. Because I'll tell you what — if I didn't know the truth, even I would have thought that two dead Hork-Bajir were about to become wolf chow.

I held my breath. Would the Yeerks be fooled? Would Visser Three believe that Rachel and I had fallen to our deaths?

I heard cruel laughter in my head. <Fools,> Visser Three sneered. <No one escapes the Yeerk

empire. Certainly not a pair of idiot Hork-Bajir. Look at them down there, all of you! That's what awaits anyone who tries to escape the Yeerks!> He laughed a terrible laugh. <The wolves will give them both the burial they deserve.>

CHAPTER 25

We waited till Visser Three and the rest of the Yeerks — human, Hork-Bajir, and Taxxons — left.

Then we crawled back up onto the lip of the ravine. We morphed back, and once we were all together again, we headed off across the land the Yeerks had burned. We knew we had to be quick. The Forest Service firefighters would be showing up soon. Even though the fire had mostly just burned itself out.

We found the valley. The lovely little valley the Ellimist had shown me. I knew what to look for. Otherwise I'd never have noticed it.

I was a good puppet for the Ellimist. I had done my job well. Not that I regretted that part of it. I could never be sorry for helping anyone escape Yeerk slavery.

But I was once more a red-tailed hawk. And so I would remain.

The entrance to the valley was so narrow the Hork-Bajir could barely fit between the rock walls. It was like some amazing bandit hideout from an old Western movie.

Jake said, "You know, I wonder if this valley even existed before."

<You think maybe the Ellimist created it?> I asked.

Jake shrugged. "Could be. It's awfully convenient."

I let it drop. I didn't really want to discuss the Ellimist. He'd lied to me. He hadn't given me back my humanity. This was a good moment for the Hork-Bajir. I wasn't going to spoil it by being selfish.

While the others squeezed through the narrow gap in the rocks, I caught a beautiful warm updraft and went up and over.

Even from the air you might not notice the valley unless you were really looking for it. From high up it just looks like a particularly dense ribbon of trees. Not until I dropped down through the branches did I see the shallow lake surrounded by sandy shores. Trees of every type and description were there. Berry bushes ringed a small, sunny meadow. The meadow I'd seen in my mind.

To tell you the truth, that little meadow would have been heaven for a red-tailed hawk. A sweet territory for a bird of prey.

I flew back to meet the others as they came into the valley. They were all standing around gaping.

"It's beautiful," Cassie breathed.

"Are we there?" Jara Hamee asked me.

<Yes. This is the place.>

"Good place," Ket Halpak said. "Good place for *kawatnoj*."

"What?" Jake asked, puzzled.

<I heard them use that word before. Jara Hamee, what does *kawatnoj* mean?>

Jara Hamee and Ket Halpak laughed their strange Hork-Bajir laugh.

"*Kawatnoj* small Hork-Bajir. Small Jara Hamee, small Ket Halpak."

"Children," Rachel translated. "They're going to have little baby Hork-Bajir."

<They will be the first Hork-Bajir born into freedom in a very long time,> Ax said. <The Ellimist did not lie. The valley exists.>

<No. He didn't lie,> I said. <Not about this, anyway.>

"Well. Let's just take our clothes off," Marco said briskly. "You know the rules — in the Garden of Eden you don't wear clothes. Rachel, you can start."

"Garden of Eden?" Jara Hamee echoed. "That is this place?"

"Not unless you want to change your name to Adam," Marco said. "I was just joking, big guy. But look, I have to know. How do you tell a male Hork-Bajir from a female?"

Jara Hamee looked puzzled. "Male? Female? What meaning?"

"Go ahead, Marco, explain," Cassie teased.

But Ket Halpak understood. "Jara Hamee and Ket Halpak different. Jara Hamee have three here." She pointed at her horn blades. "Ket have two."

"That's the only difference?" Marco asked.

"Other difference, too," Ket Halpak said primly. "But only for Hork-Bajir to know."

That got a laugh, even from Ax, which just puzzled the Hork-Bajir even more.

Everyone stayed for a little while, then they all left. All but the two Hork-Bajir and me. I stayed to help the Hork-Bajir survey their new home. I found caves where they could spend cold nights, and explained to them that they could never leave the valley. Not until Earth was rid of the Yeerks.

Then I flew home. Home to my own meadow. My own territory.

The Hork-Bajir had their Eden. The others all had their homes. I had my meadow.

CHAPTER 26

The next day was Sunday. Not that it mattered to me.

Rachel came to my meadow to see me. But I avoided her. I flew away and left her yelling, "Tobias! Tobias, where are you?" into the woods.

I'm sorry, but I knew why she was there. She'd come to tell me it would all be okay. She'd come to make sure I didn't feel too bad. And knowing Rachel, she'd help me curse and blame the Ellimist.

But I didn't want pity. Not even Rachel's pity. I was dealing with things. But I was barely dealing. And I felt like if someone was nice to me I'd totally fall apart.

I'm a predator. A raptor. A hawk. I didn't want anyone feeling sorry for me.

Throughout the day I went about my routine. I went back to mapping out the entrances to the Yeerk pool. I watched the known Controllers come and go.

And I was fine. Until the sun set and night fell. I went to my favorite perch in the old oak tree. And I watched the foxes and raccoons and owls and other night creatures do their work.

Ax came by looking for me. I didn't want to talk to him, either, but he knew I was there.

<Hey, Ax-man,> I said.

<Hello, Tobias. How are you?>

<Same as ever. And I really don't want to talk about it,> I said bluntly. I guess Ax took the hint. He stayed for just a few more seconds, then made an excuse to take off.

I knew I was just feeling sorry for myself. But too bad. I had reason to feel sorry for myself.

So this is gonna be it, I told myself bitterly. *This is your life. No home. No bed. No school. Nothing human.*

I formed a picture in my mind of human life. I saw warm golden light and a TV and couches and beds and tables. Food that came in boxes and cans. Books and magazines. Games. Stuff.

And I saw my parents. At least, the way I remembered my parents — from photographs. I'd been too young when they'd left to really be able to remember them. But I used to have pictures of them.

That was the life I would never have again. Human life.

But you know, even as I was wallowing in self-pity, I knew I was being dishonest. Maybe that warm, fuzzy, golden life was how some people lived. But it wasn't how I had lived. Not really.

Okay, I thought. *Okay, so maybe my life as a human sucked, too. That doesn't mean I want to spend the rest of my life as a bird.*

And yet I had another memory, more recent. I saw myself the way I had appeared when the Ellimist had taken me into the turquoise mist. I saw myself half-bird, half-human.

No! I said to myself. I shook off the image. Just an Ellimist trick.

I tried to stop thinking. I needed sleep. That's all. I just needed a good night's sleep. I'd be fine in the morning.

I closed my eyes and tried to turn off the busy human mind that lived alongside the hawk's simpler intelligence.

I closed my eyes . . . and when I opened them again, I was not in my tree.

I was in a room. In a house.

It was night, but I could see blue numbers glowing from an alarm clock. And I could see

157

someone lying in a narrow, disheveled bed. There was a sleeping, tousled dirty-blond head lying on the pillow.

A cold chill swept through me.

I knew this room. This bed. I knew the person lying there, tossing and turning with sad dreams.

I fluttered to the nightstand. The noise of my wings woke the sleeper.

He blinked the sleep from his eyes and stared at me. "A bird?" he said.

<It's just a dream,> I told him. My heart was beating so fast I thought it would explode. But at the same time I felt a weird calm. Like I knew what was going to happen. Like it had all happened already.

Then I saw the calendar. It was a *Star Trek* calendar. I guess that's funny. The date was the day before I had walked through the construction site with Jake and Marco and Cassie and Rachel.

"A dream?" The sleeper sat up in his bed. He peered at me and I saw a troubled expression in his eyes. "I know you, don't I?"

<Kind of,> I said. <And I know you. . . . Tobias.>

"How do you know my name?"

<I can't tell you that. But listen, Tobias, I . . .> What could I say? What could I possibly say to my old self? I couldn't tell him everything

would be all right. I didn't know that. I couldn't tell him what was about to happen to him. No sane person would believe it.

Besides, I had forgotten this dream. Hadn't I?

<Tobias,> I said. <Walk home with Jake. Walk through the construction site.>

"What?"

I just laughed a little sadly. Why had I told him to do that? Why had I sent him to the construction site? It was there that everything had begun. It was there that I had started down the path that led to my being trapped as a hawk.

I knew the truth now. I could see it clearly. I was looking at myself. Back when I was human. And looking at myself, I couldn't escape the truth — that wasn't me anymore.

I wasn't Tobias the human. I had become something else. Something new. What had the Ellimist said? ". . . you are a beginning. You are a point on which an entire time line may turn."

<Tobias?> I said to the human. <You should go back to sleep.>

"I *am* asleep, aren't I? This has to be a dream. And if it isn't a dream, I'll *never* get back to sleep!"

<I can help you sleep,> I said. <Hold out your arm. Don't be afraid.>

The human Tobias held out his arm. I flapped

my wings and landed on him. I was as gentle as I could be with my talons. I didn't need to dig them in. Simple contact was enough.

Tobias's eyes began to flutter. He became dazed and passive. The way all animals do when they are acquired.

I closed my eyes and focused on him. On the human DNA that was being absorbed into my hawk's body.

When I opened my eyes again, I was back in my tree.

Had it been real? Or was it all just some silly dream?

DON'T FORGET, a huge voice said. TWO HOURS, TOBIAS.

I didn't ask what the Ellimist meant. I knew. I had acquired my own human DNA. But it was just a morph. If I stayed in my old human body I would be trapped there forever. Never again to morph. Never again to be a hawk. Never again to fly.

HAVE I KEPT MY PROMISE?

<Yes,> I said.

AND ARE YOU HAPPY, TOBIAS?

CHAPTER 27

The next day was Monday. The day when Rachel was to receive the Packard Foundation Outstanding Student award.

There were four other kids being honored, too. They held the presentation in the school gym. Parents were there, all proud of their sons and daughters. Kids were there, having a good time, basically because the assembly got them out of last period.

I missed the early part of the ceremony. I had to be careful, you see. I had to time everything just right. There is a two-hour limit, as I know better than anyone. In that time I had to walk from the edge of the woods to the school and leave plenty of time to get back.

I was scared and nervous, sneaking into the back of the auditorium. A teacher frowned at me, like she knew me from somewhere but couldn't quite recall where.

I hung back in the shadows. The ceiling bothered me. I don't like being where I can't see the sky. But I stood there as patiently as I could, watching the ceremony through dim human eyes, and listening to the blah, blah, blah through weak human ears.

And only at the end, as the recipients filed out, did I step from the shadows.

Rachel was last in line. She was beautiful, as always. And she had the usual Rachel swagger.

I saw Cassie give her a wink as she walked by. Rachel rolled her eyes, self-mocking, and Cassie laughed.

When she passed by where Marco was sitting, Marco made a phony bow. You know, like he was bowing before some idol. Rachel laughed and shook her head.

And then she was right there in front of me. I saw her eyes sweep over me, indifferent, and then look past me toward the door.

She stopped walking.

She turned to me. Her eyes were wide.

"Hi, Rachel," I said with a human voice.

#14 The Unknown

"Hey. Is that the horse you're looking for?" Rachel asked.

"Where?"

"There. Back by the road. Back by that pay phone."

My dad and I turned back to look. A scruffy roan horse was swaying from side to side as it walked. Swaying like a drunk.

As we watched, the horse seemed to be attracted to the telephone. It picked up the receiver with its mouth and let it hang off the hook.

And that's when things got strange. The horse lowered its head to the ground, picked up a twig in its lips, and seemd to be poking the telephone keyboard.

"Am I crazy, or is that horse trying to make a phone call?" Rachel said.

My dad shrugged. "Must be disoriented. Doesn't know what it's doing. Come on, let's get over there."

I dropped behind a few steps to fall in with Rachel.

"That horse is dialing the phone," Rachel said in a whisper.

"Sure looks like it," I agreed.

"Ordering a pizza?" Rachel suggested.

"Hay, alfalfa, and extra cheese?"

My dad was getting close to the horse. The horse spotted him, and hesitated. Like it wanted to complete its phone call. But also wanted to run away. It decided to run. Only it wasn't really up for running. The best it could do was wobble off into the darkness, practically falling over as it went.

"Whoa, girl, whoa," my dad said in his calming-the-animals voice. "Whoa. I'm just try-ing to help you."

Suddenly I noticed something happening to the horse's head. "Look!" I whispered.

There, crawling its way out of the horse's left ear, was a slug. A large, gray slug.

"Is that what I think it is?" Rachel whispered.

"Yeah. I think so."

The gray slug wormed its way out of the horse's head. It plopped heavily on the gravel and grass beneath it. And then it started to writhe away.

I'd seen those slugs before. We both had.

"Yeerk," I whispered. "There was a Yeerk in this horse."

Don't miss **the andalite chronicles**

We led Loren over to our fighter, and then we carried the second human across. He was unconscious. Bright red blood ran from a cut above his left eye.

<Red blood?> Arbron said. <*Red? Yuck.*>

I was trying to act more mature than Arbron, but to tell you the truth, blood that color creeped me out, too. Still, I didn't think humans looked ugly or anything. Not like the Skrit or Taxxons, which are seriously ugly species. Nor did they look dangerous, like the Hork-Bajir.

Mostly they looked funny. I'd never seen a species that walked on just two legs without even a tail to help with balance. Arbron said what I was thinking. <All it would take is one little push and they'd fall right over. Earth must be hysterical! Humans falling forward and back, falling all over the place. No wonder they are so primitive. They probably spend all their time just trying to stand up.>

We were almost back to the Dome ship when the second human woke up. We'd left the Skrit Na to try to figure out how to fix their ship. That was their problem.

Hey, no one told them to shoot at us. Right?

"Unh," the human moaned.

He was larger than Loren. Maybe two or three inches larger. His hair was brown, not golden, and it was cut short. His eyes were also brown, not blue like Loren's.

Loren went to him and bent her legs in such a way that she could kneel down beside him. Arbron and I exchanged a look of amazement. It had to be hard to kneel like that and not fall.

"Hey, kid, you okay?" Loren asked.

The wounded human opened his eyes and blinked. He stared hard at me. "What happened?"

Loren shrugged. "Now we have a different bunch of aliens. Who'da guessed there were so many people zipping around outer space? Are you okay? That big cockroach popped you pretty good back there."

<You have nothing to fear,> I said gently. <You are safe now.>

The human felt his wound and looked at the red blood. He seemed almost as grossed out as I was. But he climbed to his feet. Which involved using his hands, I noticed. Humans seem to have stronger hands than we have.

<I am Elfangor. This is Arbron. We are Andalites. We will return you to your home planet.>

The human nodded slowly. "Telepathy. You use telepathy to talk." His gaze traveled to my stalk eyes, back to my face, then to my tail. "That tail is a weapon, isn't it? Is it poisonous or does it just cut?"

I decided right then that I didn't like this human as much as Loren. I didn't like him much at all. <I politely told you my name, human,> I said coldly. <Now, I require *your* name.>

The human gave me a look that seemed insolent. Although who can really tell what an alien facial expression means?

"My name is Hedrick, actually. But I prefer my last name. Most people call me by my last name: Chapman."

"I think these Andalites are okay," Loren said to Chapman. "At least they're better-looking than the last bunch. And they've promised to —"

"Shut up," Chapman snapped. "I'm not interested in the opinion of a kid."

"Kid? Hey, you big jerk, who was it that got the weapon after the ship stopped moving? *Me*. And who was it that was cringing in the back, begging for mercy? *You*. And anyway, I'd be surprised if you're even a year older than me."

Chapman's face grew pink. A fascinating thing to watch. He clenched his jaw tightly. "And now it seems your heroics were pointless. We're prisoners again. And I have a feeling we won't be grabbing guns away from these Andalites."

Suddenly, he lunged forward toward the Dracon beam in my hand! Without even thinking, I whipped my tail forward and pressed the blade against Chapman's throat.

Chapman laughed. "See that? See how fast he was? Couldn't even see that tail move." Again he gave me an insolent look. "What did you say your species is called? Andalites? Well, I have a feeling you guys are a little more dangerous than you pretend to be, despite all your polite talk and promises."

I felt like a fool. Not for the first time that day. The human Chapman had been testing me.

<We need to prepare to dock with the Dome ship,> Arbron reminded me.

I went through the docking procedure, moving the fighter back inside the fighter bay. I concentrated on my work, but I was upset. I didn't like the human named Chapman. I didn't like his suspicion toward me. After all, we had rescued him from a future as a zoo animal on the Skrit Na home world. He should be grateful.

But maybe that's the way humans are. I've heard there are species that can't handle anyone helping them. They'd rather die than ever be in debt to someone.

But judging by Loren, not all humans were that way.

Not your problem, Elfangor, I told myself. *Just turn the humans over to the captain. Not your problem at all.*

But I was wrong. The humans *were* my problem.

In fact, I was about to have lots of problems.

Cassie learns the hard way...
Never underestimate
the power of a morph

ANIMORPHS

My hindquarters bunched up and fired every muscle fiber at once. And before I knew what was happening, I was running. But not running away. I ran straight for the first Hork-Bajir.

"HrrrEEEEE-HEEE-he-he!" I reared up, all the way back until I was standing on my hind legs, and I flailed madly with my forehooves.

I couldn't exactly aim my hooves, mind you. Horses aren't predators. But I flailed away and just as the Hork-Bajir was pressing the trigger...

ANIMORPHS #14: THE UNKNOWN

COMING IN DECEMBER!

K.A. Applegate

Everything is changing all over again....